VEGAN LEATHER

Sarah Hampton

2QT Publishing

First Edition published 2025 by
2QT Publishing
United Kingdom

Vegan Leather is a work of fiction and any resemblance
to any person living or dead is purely coincidental

Cover image: © Adobe Stock
Printed by IngramSpark

A CIP catalogue record for this book is available
from the British Library

ISBN 978-1-7385640-5-7

Dedication

To forebears who told it as it was.

Acknowledgements

To Karen Holmes my continual thanks for her friendship, encouragement and editorial wisdom. Thank you to Catherine Cousins and Hilary Pitt who have patiently guided me towards publication of this final novel.

Gratitude to Patrick Hanks and Simeon Potter for publishing the *Hamlyn Encyclopedic World Dictionary*, 1971. Its definitions have remained a constant and reliable source of reference.

The author's previous titles:

Learning to Tie a Bow
Picking at the Knot
Searching for a Marlinspike

Out of the night that covers me,
  Black as the pit from pole to pole,
I thank whatever gods may be
  For my unconquerable soul.

In the fell clutch of circumstance
  I have not winced nor cried aloud.
Under the bludgeonings of chance
  My head is bloody, but unbowed.

Beyond this place of wrath and tears
  Looms but the Horror of the shade,
And yet the menace of the years
  Finds and shall find me unafraid.

It matters not how strait the gate,
  How charged with punishments the scroll,
I am the master of my fate,
  I am the captain of my soul.

William Ernest Henley

CHAPTER I

The old order changeth giving way to… But of course, that had been the problem: no one had explained that a cultural shift of seismic proportions could happen so quickly. Observa had assumed that her values would be absorbed and carried on by those who came after her, briefly questioned then passed to the next generation.

Was God still out there, pricking people's consciences, however irrelevant He had become? All those centuries believing England was a Christian nation with state and church intertwined. Henry VIII had seen to that; he must have had a purpose in all that cleansing and destruction.

The dissolution of the monasteries had stuck in Observa's mind, and she had attempted to pass on the relevance of that cultural shift in an earlier century to her children, grandchildren and great-grandchildren.

She remembered the trudge over the fields to Shap Abbey before the days when she'd had a car, the children complaining that they were too hot. Days out with a picnic to Fountains Abbey; when hide-and-seek among the ruins had flagged, there were the stepping stones across the river at Bolton Abbey. It was an adventure when the river was in spate, the water cascading over the stones, mini waterfalls making them almost invisible and slippery for bare feet.

They used to sing 'Sunwac, sunwac, sunwac', the mnemonic for the rivers of Yorkshire. Now she couldn't remember if Bolton Abbey was on the Nidd or the Wharfe.

She liked to suppose that those attempts at home schooling had borne fruit in some way, been instrumental in guiding her elder daughter towards higher education, because it had made her feel less of a failure on the parenting front. Her daughter's latest novel about the dissolution of the monasteries had reached the best-seller lists, garnered positive reviews, and there was the possibility of some award.

Why did certain things harbour in your mind whilst others of more significance were washed out to sea into the uncharted waters of dementia? She had been pondering these thoughts for quite some time before the end came and now they were still with her as she drifted around in what, as a believer, she assumed to be Heaven. Presumably those of a scientific and secular disposition were elsewhere.

Whilst her mind and body had still been one, she had kept her thoughts to herself. Mothers and God knew never to discuss religion or politics in polite society; that had been one of the mantras of her upbringing.

The state called upon the clergy from time to time to

add a bit of gravitas on ceremonial occasions, provide a theatrical backdrop, but within the blink of an eyelid trust had turned to treachery. The media, now omnipotent, spewed out its salacious untruths to nurture mistrust and uncertainty. A new high priest had been proclaimed and he shall be called Tik Tok.

God had eventually been ignored, but those who have been ignored seek retribution and now mankind had had its chance. She should have spoken out. Was it too late?

She could speak her thoughts now because there was no one left to listen. Friends and family were gone; weakened by Covid, they had succumbed to the plague and the civil unrest that had followed.

She suspected there might be one or two survivors who had taken to their beds to await the end, those of her vintage who had lived through wars and deprivation and reached their centenary with an understanding of the word 'thrift'. Still hanging on to the lessons of self-reliance and human responsibility learned at their mothers' knees before they were supplanted by human rights and Me, Me, Me. Out of sight, out of mind had become the new mantra. Ignorance was bliss…

She had risked it, gone outside to walk the two hundred yards up to the top gate because she needed to be there one last time, to lean on a gate she had latched, unlatched and passed through a thousand times. She needed to gaze one final time at the landscape, weep one last time for its beauty and intimacy and mourn its memories, for she was unsure what the afterlife would have in store.

She no longer feared the packs of feral dogs that roamed free. They had quickly sussed the situation when their human masters had succumbed to the virus and gnawed through their leashes to escape their oppressive, mawkish domesticity. Many of the dogs were victims themselves, traded on Facebook as the latest must-haves, but now their hunting instincts were muzzle free.

It had taken her some time to reach the gate. Her old body could only shuffle along, and nature had reclaimed the land. The paddock where sheep had once safely grazed was now waist high in brambles, thistles, dockings and uncropped fescues and sedges.

In previous years a neighbouring farmer had lent her an elderly cow to eat off the grasses. For the past six or seven years, a succession of Daisies had nurtured their last calves and spent their final, idyllic summer with her among the harebells and rattle grass.

It had been the ideal setting for man and beast to see out their days. The cows, assured of their destiny, knew that when the leaves turned golden and started to drop they would be taken away in a wagon as their contemporaries had been, a kindly word spoken 'there you go, old girl', and an affectionate pat on their rumps as they went up the ramp, oblivious that in a few weeks' time they would return to the shelves of the local supermarket, tinned and labelled as gourmet food for cats and dogs.

In cow years the last Daisy had been of similar age to Observa, whose future after death was less certain. Daisy would lumber to the gate to say hello, limping because her legs were giving her pain, asking to have her neck scratched. In return she would lick Observa's face with that reassuring sandpaper tongue Observa remembered from childhood.

It had been a time of contentment for both of them, nirvana to bring to an end life's experiences – that is until it was interrupted and people started knocking on the door. Videos of Daisy struggling across the garth had gone viral. Ramblers clutching their smartphones, no longer interested in the scenery, were now into animal welfare and had reported her.

Observa imagined that had she been raised as a Hindu she would be reunited with the souls of millions of cows; their souls would be all around her under the protection of Lord Krishna

Her hips had been too arthritic for her to lift her legs over the twisted dry grasses that had plaited together to snare her shuffling feet.

Her father had taught her many of the names of the grasses, made a game of it, chosen those with names that would fire her imagination and invite her questions: rattle grass; couch grass; sheep's fescue; bladder sedge; crested dog's tail. She had never thanked him sufficiently for all that love and guidance.

She had thought of returning to the barn to find a sickle with which to slash her way through but, like her, it would be blunted by age. A sound came back to her, metal on stone: Father sharpening a sickle on a watering stone. Quick flicks of the wrist, sparks flying as he put an edge to the blade in the same way he sharpened the knife to carve the Sunday joint.

Father always carved the meat for with that task came privilege, his fingers ripping off the crisp parson's nose of a chicken and the prolonged 'uuuummmmm' of pleasure. When a trout he had caught was on the menu, he would carefully remove the oyster from behind its gill; he called it the fisherman's bite.

Observa had been within grabbing distance of the gate, but if she fell there would be no way of getting up again. Before the plague, she had worn an emergency button on a strap around her wrist. If she had a tumble, she pressed the button and was put through to a detached voice of a person based in Folkestone who kindly alerted someone in the village to go and pick her up. Now no one answered the phone and, as far as she knew, there were no survivors in the village. The young and middle-aged had died first, their immune systems weakened by easy living and health-and-safety directives.

The dogs would sense a weakened prey and be on her in a minute. Perhaps it would be the easier way to go; a quick bite to her throat by the leading hound would be preferable to lying frozen and starving in bed.

Arm outstretched, she had steadied herself and clutched the top rail tightly, leaning on it to catch her breath. It had been hung in a hurry centuries earlier, balanced incorrectly on the rusty leaden crooks of a bygone age that had been welded into the rough stone stoop, and used too hastily by those who came afterwards.

She remembered one of her father's quotes: 'It's as daft

as a yat et swings beath ways.' He had enjoyed reverting to his Cumbrian dialect when he was with her.

How fortunate she had been to have him for a father. Had she thanked him sufficiently at the time for all that companionship? But it wouldn't be long before she met up with him again. She was certain that he was still out there somewhere because he sent her messages, his thoughts breaking into hers from time to time.

Jokingly, she had blamed him for the names her brothers had called her. He had said that of all his children she was the most observant and had given her the pet name Observa. Her brothers had resented this and started calling her 'Obby', which quickly turned to Gobby. They had taunted her with that nickname until, as the years passed, the teasing became affectionate and she had accepted it with a smile.

She had raised her eyes one last time to the hills and the carpet of autumn-gold bracken turned pink by the disappearing western sun. She had twisted to retrace her steps, but when she pushed the gate open she did not use enough force and it swung back, knocking her to the ground.

Her fall had been cushioned by the undergrowth, but in the distance she could hear hounds giving tongue and she swore at her own stupidity. 'Shit, shit, shit – you bloody stupid old woman,' she muttered, then she laughed.

She was disappointed in herself but she would never indulge in self-pity; it was a rather unpleasant trait that had recently become a national pastime in which she had no wish to participate.

Lying on the ground was not how she had wished to leave this earth, but trying to push herself up would only have wearied her further; she could not rely on the gate, which was swinging free.

She'd had no idea how long she might last. 'You've had a good innings,' her friends would have said. But what was the point of a good innings if the runs you made counted for nought, didn't go up on the score board and were deemed 'no balls' by the generations that followed?

It was beginning to get dark; the sun had disappeared and she could feel the creeping cold. They said that when you were dying the whole of your life flashed in front of you, but who were *they* and how could they know? Since the risen Christ, had there been other recordings? Unless – unless there really was an afterlife.

She had started to feel more positive. Her body relaxed and she felt less cold…

When the electricity had gone off, she had thought it was just the usual temporary breakdown, a familiar blip in remote rural areas, but keeping track of time without power had become a struggle as the hours rolled into days and the days rolled into weeks. She had managed to keep the grandfather clock going with its reassuring tick until her wrists had become too weak to wind up the heavy lead weights.

The tinned food lasted longer than she'd anticipated,

and she supplemented it with plants from the hedgerows that were familiar from her wartime childhood days – hips, haws, nettles, sorrel and roots of all kinds. But eventually things became more challenging.

Had she been younger she would have coped, but frailty and lack of balance were her enemies and they had made it difficult to collect fallen branches and sticks to keep the wood-burning stove alight. Before it was all used up, there had been a pile of dried-out peat sods, cut when the family had rights of turbary on the fell before the environmentalists put a stop to self-sufficiency. Wood-burning stoves had been banned years ago in order to save the planet, but there was no one around now to give her a criminal record.

She needed to go and check the stove. She might be in luck because occasionally a pigeon fell down the chimney and alerted her with its telltale fluttering.

Once upon a time she would have rescued it, felt its pounding heart in her hand, flicked the soot from it and carried it to the back door to be released on the wind with an 'off you go'. Now she waited until the fluttering stopped, reached for the Swan Vestas and lit the feathers, her arthritic hands grateful that they had not been asked to pluck it. A restaurant would have described the flesh as raw to medium.

Loneliness was never a problem, and she had adapted well to the cold, never removing her nine or ten layers of clothing in winter. The three woollen, long-sleeved vests full of holes, which had belonged to Mother, were her permanent undergarments. They had been made by

Brettles and still bore their wartime utility mark.

When the longing to experience warmth, however fleeting, became overwhelming, she allowed the contents of her bladder to trickle down her legs but the blissful five seconds only intensified the bitter cold that followed.

The days grew shorter; the nettles, now her main source of food, were dying back and she was worried about finding an alternative. The answer had come from an unexpected quarter whilst she was searching through a little-used chest of drawers hoping to find discarded batteries that might still contain a flicker of life.

At the back of the bottom drawer was a small box, Fortnum and Mason on the lid, containing old photos and short handwritten letters with embossed addresses. She would have to wait for tomorrow's daylight before she could read them.

It was ironic that now she had all the time in the world to read, she was unable to do so. She had planned a dotage renewing her acquaintance with Dickens, Shakespeare, the Lakeland poets and all the boys in the band – perhaps more importantly the Bible, which she had neglected for far too long. But her eyes were failing and she had to ration their use, just as she needed to ration the last of the candles that must be saved for the long, dark, winter evenings that might lie ahead.

Matches she had aplenty; she had found a cache of Swan Vestas in a kitchen drawer, their familiar green, red and white logo somehow reassuring. It reminded her of those idyllic holidays in Italy when living was good, although even then people knew the good could not last.

She could see the photos. One was a small sepia snapshot of a couple emerging arm in arm from an imposing building, he in officer's army uniform, she in a suit and a jaunty hat carrying a posy of flowers.

It was a picture she had never seen before but she recognised the people: it was her brother-in-law's wedding day. He had married in haste shortly after his release from a German prisoner-of-war camp. The union had caused friction because the bride wearing the jaunty hat had not been welcomed into the family fold by her in-laws. She was not what they had in mind for the elder son and heir.

Jacoba was Dutch and of colonial descent; comments at the time included 'a touch of the tar brush'. Observa had got on quite well with her; they had shared intimacies and she had tried to lessen the obvious antagonism shown by her in-laws. When they had introduced their daughters-in-law, they would almost ignore Jacoba whilst Observa was introduced as 'the mother of our grandchildren' before friendly social chat ensued.

It had been a rubbing of salt into an open wound. Jacoba had confided the reason for her childlessness. In the last year of the Nazi occupation, the people of Holland were starving and had stayed alive by eating their national asset, tulip bulbs. Because of malnutrition she had never menstruated. Years later she said, 'Perhaps it was a good thing.'

Why had she, Observa, not thought of tulip bulbs before? All those carefully selected ones in the herbaceous border that had given such pleasure over the years, the hours drooling over the bulb catalogues in that other life. Friends called it 'horticultural porn'. Would it be sacrilege to eat the bulbs and not allow them to greet another spring?

Finally she decided to dig around with a short fork in one of the pots in which, some years earlier, she had planted a mixture of pale yellow, pale purple and pink bulbs. They were part of the Princes Collection and she tried to remember their individual names.

Holding tight to the rim of the pot to keep her balance, she extracted four bulbs and washed them in a puddle in the yard. Unsure how palatable they would be, she chopped them to pulp and swallowed them.

The television signal had remained active far longer than she had anticipated, but when it finally flickered and the images disappeared, she was relieved. Those images over the last few years had become disturbing: civil unrest, arson, looting, stabbings and crowds of feral urban youths plundering the countryside. Five-year-olds in the playground exchanging violent games on their Smartphones, prisoners of Midas sitting in Castle Silicon. Mothers re-learning the forgotten words of lullabies to drown out the sounds of war at bedtime.

Was it Luke or Matthew – or both – who had said something about 'those who shall cause one of these little ones who believe in me to sin, it were better for him that a millstone were hanged about his neck'? There was a millstone somewhere in the garden, left by the previous owners, gathering moss.

How long, long, long ago were the playgrounds of her

youth: Winnie the Pooh; hopscotch and exchanging cigarette cards decorated with the kings and queens of England; wild flowers, butterflies and dogs. Her brothers had collected footballers, cricketers and cars, unaware that the product the cards promoted as 'clear as a mountain stream' were probably killing their parents.

Other species had tried to issue warnings: three hundred pilot whales had beached on a paradise island. There were numerous scientists willing to give an opinion, but Observa was unlikely to be asked for hers; she had no qualifications other than that she had spoken out when the environmental experts sold offshore windfarms to a gullible public with little thought about how they might affect the country's marine neighbours.

'We don't want those huge pulsating humming things in our back yard, stick 'em in the sea.'

Her reservations were pooh-poohed. 'Oh, she's got another bee in her bonnet. She's going a bit senile and she's always been sceptical about the green movement.'

She could hear a pack of dogs baying nearby, a familiar, comforting sound from her childhood when she'd followed the hounds, but when these started howling she knew that they had caught her scent. The noise reminded her of the air-raid sirens during WW2 – or was it WW3?

✳

If there were an afterlife, how would she know that she was physically dead? She imagined it would be like changing stations on a long train journey, a manoeuvre she had always anticipated with alarm and dread.

She had no idea how long she lay there as the darkness came and went. She could feel the brambles on her hands and ankles, their thorns taking hold of her. She had read somewhere that there were 290 different species of bramble, so it wouldn't take them long to engulf the planet. How pleased those Extinction Rebellion people would have been had they still been around.

She was falling in and out of consciousness. What day was it? She was certain that she could hear the jingle-jangle of the ice-cream van announcing its presence, so it must be Friday evening. Mr Slee would be parked on the corner waiting for his usual customers, but when she listened more closely the sound was more like a call to prayer and she distinctly heard the words 'Allahu Akbar'.

When she awoke, she was hovering ten or perhaps twenty feet above the earth, looking down upon herself.

Chapter 2

Observa had had similar experiences before in clinical surroundings. Once someone had patted her hand and said her name. 'Are you still with us? Come back to us, dear.' And she had, but not before she'd caught a glimpse of herself lying prostrate on a hospital bed, a bird's eye view of a detached body that no longer belonged to her.

Now there was no one holding her hand and she had no wish to go back.

It took her some time to realise where she was and what had precipitated her being there. One moment she had been standing at the gate, thanking it for its memories and thinking that every prospect pleases and only man is vile – how those Victorian hymn writers had hit the nail on the head – and now her mind was in a different place. It was suspended above the ground, looking down on a crumpled form lying among the brambles, its face obscured by thistles and long, wilting grasses.

The clothes were familiar: mustard-coloured moleskins and Hunter wellies with a split up the side. How she had loved her yellow moleskins; they had been expensive and their purchase was out of character, but they had been worth every penny for the confidence they had given her. Old friends who used to phone remembered them. She had bought them whilst staying with one of her daughters.

The flashbacks were coming thick and fast. She was little again, two- or three-ish, at the beginning of awareness. She was sitting in the front seat of Father's old maroon bull-nosed Morris with its reassuring smell of wet leather and the sound of double-declutching. She wasn't wearing a seat belt; this was before the health-and-safety industry had been invented, before the word 'misadventure' had been erased from the nation's vocabulary and been replaced by the word 'blame'.

She remembered her father's words vividly. He had waved to someone standing by a farm gate and commented, 'If it's a Ramsey, smile.'

Too small at the time to see out of the side windows or the windscreen, and too young to understand the significance of his comment, his instruction had remained unquestioned until she was about ten when father had explained the importance of smiling. His advice was never of a practical nature but always of sound value: 'Smile, even though you know that the recipient is unlikely to return the compliment.'

It was a wisdom that had carried her through life, though she had taken on board that sometimes a smiley face could disguise evil intent. Life was just a question of double-declutching until you found the right gear.

It must have been about that time, when she was still

at primary school waiting to be 'sent away to widen her education', that she became aware that ladies liked her father. They held his arm and kissed him on the cheek when they hardly knew him, and they smiled at him a lot, especially Mrs Crowhurst who taught arithmetic at school. Mrs Crowhurst was very pretty and the pupils had crushes on her.

Because Observa was hopeless at arithmetic, it was mooted that extra tuition might help. Acting as a go-between, she suggested asking Mrs Crowhurst to tea; there did not appear to be a Mr Crowhurst. Mother said what a good idea and sent her a little note.

It was a Sunday and Father was at home. Within fifteen minutes, Mrs Crowhurst had slipped her arm through Father's as they walked across the lawn. They didn't look as though they were discussing mathematics.

Mother, who was never judgemental and good at shrugging things off, saw only the good in people; her philosophy was 'there but for the grace of God go I'. On being informed that Father had been seen kissing Mrs Crowhurst, her reply had been, 'How nice.' Then she had added, 'I suspect it was Mrs Crowhurst kissing your father,' and that was the end of the matter. Arithmetic tuition was forgotten and long division remained a lifelong mystery.

Mother's wisdom came from deep inside her. Her advice was of a practical nature, such as 'never take sweets from strangers', though some of the things she said were confusing. Reared on Quaker beliefs, she had switched track on meeting Father. Her brothers were both conscientious objectors but had done their bit nursing the wounded with the Friends' ambulance service in France, whereas Father had been in the firing line.

It was some years later, when they were washing up in the kitchen, that Mother had announced that it was a pity that Hitler had not invaded England. She had qualified the statement by saying, 'It would have done us good, and we would not be feeling this sense of entitlement that seems to have taken hold. A dose of occupation might have united us.'

Thank goodness Mother and Father had died when they did. How they would have hated social media with its messages of mistrust. Its insidious culture had settled like a pyroclastic dust. It had choked thought and engulfed the mind until the ability to look someone straight in the eye and shake their hand firmly to confirm that their word was their bond had almost disappeared; a quick swipe sufficed.

The Internet had started out so well, a kind of enlightenment that had brought knowledge to the people of the world. The trouble was that the warnings of original sin were sidelined by Silicon Valley. It was already too late when people started to realise what was being done to them; they were busy trying to save the planet by going on marches and disrupting traffic whilst holding the real enemy in their hands. Along with many other words 'enlightenment' had lost its way and been shortened, its consonants confused to become 'entitlement'.

Many words had lost their true meaning so that it had sometimes been difficult to communicate with the young.

Observa had tried to explain the meaning of the word 'thrift', of which they had no understanding.

Memory had taken a back seat. To be remembered was to still exist, of that she was certain, and she was sure that she would find her father and mother however limitless the universe. It was just a question of getting on the right wavelength but, as she had never got as far as having a physics lesson she would have to rely on instinct, one of the things Father had said she possessed.

Where to start? If she could persuade her mind to take itself to where Father had died, he might well be hovering above the Somerset Levels, forced to spend his final days in an old people's home far from his beloved roots because it had been more convenient for certain members of the family to put him there. If his mind had taken him to where he wished to be, he would be closer to home, drifting and rejoicing above the hills of the north. He shouldn't be too hard to find.

Perhaps now was the time to try out some thought transference, something, together with telepathy, in which Observa had always believed. Faith would do the rest. Perhaps in outer space minds became magnetic and attracted others of the same ilk...

Just thinking about her father made her feel his presence. She had kept some of his personal possessions, they had been left behind in that other life to be thrown into a skip, unread and unvalued.

When she had been able to hold them in her hand, they had meant so much to her. She had felt the strength in the small, battered, leather-bound prayer book, the gold-leaf lettering on the cover long since dimmed, so worn that the only decipherable letters were the capital C and P for Common Prayer.

But the confident message written in ink in a bold hand inside the cover was clear: *To Arthur – with Mother's love* and the date, *November, 1913*. It must have been Father's confirmation gift, the last present his mother had given him because she had died a few months later. Three years later he had volunteered for war. It would be nice to fantasise that he had kept it on his person at all times and that was why he had survived.

No generation was prepared for the end. It crept up like grandmother's footsteps, the gradual slowing down until one morning you woke up and realised that your hour had come; life was at its end and you asked yourself, 'Was that it?' All those mistakes and wrong turns and thoughts that 'next time I shall do things differently', but the way ahead had signs saying 'road closed' and there were no diversion notices. Getting things right tomorrow was no longer an option; better concentrate on the good times. And when you looked at the lives of others, you realised just how fortunate you had been.

Of course, you had to ask yourself what was all that about. What on earth was the point of all that stress? What were 'things' – and how did one get them right? Just trying to be happy should do it.

Had life been normal, funerals would still have been happening and people still dying in a civilised way. Observa had arranged for a recording of Sting singing 'Spread a Little Happiness as Years Go By' at her own departure to remind any remaining family and friends of its importance. She could well imagine the tut-tutting.

Being right about any subject was questionable because people had been told that only at the day of judgement would the truth be known. In her day there had been 'soothsayers' – men of letters, elder statesmen – one a classicist who spoke Greek. He had translated a passage as a warning to his fellow countrymen and was ridiculed for his prophecies, howled down by the mob that was still shouting for Barabbas.

Had he spoken in Greek, there would have been no furore.

✳

Observa was starting to enjoy the afterlife, seeing things face to face and not through a glass darkly, though she knew that she must keep an open mind and build on the wisdom and perception she had garnered during her life on earth.

Wisdom had become an unfashionable word that belonged to the elderly, and the elderly were unnecessary and a drain on the country's resources. Image was everything: show affection to a cat or dog, and you instantly became an exemplary human being.

Words had lost their true meaning and been trivialised; some had been expunged. 'Decency' had said it all: conformity to the recognised standards of propriety, good taste and modesty, but 'propriety' was struggling, and 'modesty' had long since been replaced by vanity.

No, she didn't want to go back to the drip-drip of man-made catastrophes because she had found it difficult to witness the mistakes that were being made.

Her upbringing had taught her to see only the good in people, and her nurturing close to nature had given her pride in her values. Now, however, Piers Plowman no longer held sway; those who understood the earth were made to take a back seat and listen to writers with too much to say.

A fox was approaching her body.

Chapter 3

Where was everyone? Surely if this were Heaven it should be chock-a-block, but no one was about and she was unsure of the protocol. Was there a welcoming committee? The brochure had not been specific and she was uncertain who would make the final decision on her future. Would it be her maker or an intermediary – St Peter, perhaps. She had always liked what he had to say, and the look of him since seeing those icons at St Catherine's Monastery below Mount Sinai during a holiday in the Middle East. He'd had a kindly face.

Observa wondered how far above the ground she was hovering. She assumed that she was floating in the solar system, the other side of the moon as promised in fairy tales – although fairy tales did not always have happy endings. Well, at least she would not have to reserve a seat on a space shuttle; all you needed was the patience to die and you were finally transported free of charge.

Was she in the stratosphere, the troposphere or the ionosphere? It was rather like going to the theatre: would there be a better view from the gods or the front stalls?

Her priority was to find her family and, if she were fortunate, one of those interesting men who had whispered in her ear, 'You know that I love you.' She had not believed them, but she would still like to know if any of them had made it to Heaven.

Did she need to join a queue, like those queues of migrants from yesteryear crossing the Channel and waiting to hear what border control had decided, or the shuffling crocodile of Jews trustingly waiting at the gates of hell at Auschwitz, Belsen and Buchenwald? And how did you make contact with those who had gone before? There was no instruction manual but surely it shouldn't be difficult; she had always been good at picking up vibes and could sense distress in others.

She tried calling to the body lying on the ground but she had no voice. Frustrated, she tried to bite her bottom lip but her lips were no longer part of her even though she could see them. They had turned blue.

The fox was approaching cautiously. It stopped once or twice and lifted its head to listen, aware of the baying hounds in the distance. It started gnawing on the lower part of her body and she saw her thigh through a tear in her mustard moleskins. How she had loved those trousers, had felt good in them. They had not had a pair in her size and she had been encouraged to buy a larger one; they had needed a belt to keep them up.

She had bought them at a smart boutiquey shop in Burford during one of those enjoyable stays in Oxford with her daughter. Her northern caution had flinched at the price but they had been good value, lasted well and adapted to her shape over the years. Even when they were threadbare and the knees were almost through, she had continued to wear them.

Her daughters must be up here somewhere because they had beaten her to it, was it two years ago? Both high flyers weakened by Covid, they had succumbed quickly to the plague that followed. It had been distressing, but daughters dying before their mothers had become commonplace over the last few decades.

✳

Naturally, she had argued with her children, two generations clashing as new cultures were introduced before lessons were learned from the old ones.

'God is mumbo-jumbo,' one of her daughters had told her. 'Only weak-minded people would believe such rubbish.' It had hurt, but to prolong the discussion, to try and explain faith, would only have made things worse.

Heavens! As non-believers, her daughters might not be here! Surely they wouldn't have been sent to the other place? Her God would not allow such prejudice and discrimination, would recognise that they had ticked all the right boxes on earth and their kindness to others far outweighed their earthly duty to Him. But, of course, He had also said, 'Vengeance is mine.'

They had been wonderful daughters and how she had loved them, been so proud of their achievements, but they were so, so different. The older one was petite and mousey, with nondescript straight hair and freckled skin.

She faded into the wallpaper on social occasions – until you were introduced to her brain; she could effortlessly hold the attention of a hundred students in a lecture theatre.

The younger one caught the eye wherever she went. Tall, big boned like her father's side of the family, with a mass of shiny black hair and perfect skin, her appearance would bring a room at a party to silence when she walked in – but if she was asked to make a public statement or take the chair, she declined.

Behind the scenes their contribution to humanity had been immense but, like many before them, had gone unrecognised. People used to make comments – 'Have they the same father?' – and when they thought Observa was out of earshot murmur, 'A bit of straying in the past?'

She hadn't minded; she had thought it rather amusing.

The sun was behind her and she noticed she was casting no shadow. All her life Observa had been afraid of her own shadow; now she appeared not to have one and she felt relief. The wearisome dominance of her body had been expunged; her head had been given its freedom and was now in charge.

A vixen arrived to join the dog fox and tentatively tugged at Observa's lower lip. They lifted their heads frequently to listen for predators, knowing instinctively the moment to run for cover. The dogs were almost upon them, turning upon one another because they had yet to regain their natural instinct and learn to hunt as a pack.

She recognised a few of them because they had belonged to people in the village. Pippa the guide dog, all instinct knocked out of her, taught never to run or chase a ball and always to walk slowly; she was not participating but standing on the fringe of the pack, unsure of her loyalties and maybe her species.

And there was dear old George. Observa had left the door open and said goodbye to him when they both knew death was inevitable. She had told him to go but he had remained at her side, bless him, until hunger overcame him.

There was Bob, the vicar's Jack Russell, a friendly dog that she had admired. He was so familiar in a different setting, his head between his paws as he waited patiently whilst she and his master put the world to rights over a cup of coffee at her kitchen table, his eyes passing from one to the other as though he understood every word. Now he looked self-assured and was standing up to Sam, the hyperactive cocker spaniel who was a menace and into everything. Like his owner, Jack, his tail never stopped wagging.

A couple of designer dogs were trying to regain their mongrel strength. She had seen them being walked in the village; they had probably belonged to second-home owners. Now set free from the imprisonment of domesticity, they appeared unsure. They had been bred for their looks; they would soon succumb when it came to survival of the fittest.

✳

Observa was finding that her mind was free to go its own way. If that was what the Bible meant by rising from the dead, it was becoming an interesting and absorbing challenge and she was starting to feel more confident. Perhaps the mind was programmed only to function at full capacity after death, like the stages of those slow-release medicines.

Could it be that the souls of the dead stayed in close proximity to the place where they had left the body? If she could take her mind back to the locations where people had died, she might bump into them – not literally, of course, but if she thought about them sufficiently perhaps she could catch their attention and attract their minds. Should they, by coincidence, fate or faith, happen to be thinking of her the attraction of minds would be magnetic.

She decided that she would start with Father. She was beginning to feel quite excited; maybe death really was an awfully big adventure.

Chapter 4

Until that moment, she had never thought about atonement; the word had only been given resonance when she randomly opened her diary at the month of September. It was one of those diaries that sidetracked you with exquisite plant illustrations on the adjoining page, making you forget what it was you were looking for.

It was the italics that caught her eye: *Day of Atonement, Yom Kippur.* She had opened the diary to record her next visit to the dentist but instead Googled Yom Kippur, although she had no idea why.

Her brain was having its familiar struggle with right and wrong, and the sense of needing to atone for something was becoming stronger. In her former life, she had repeated her general confession more times than she cared to remember: 'We have left undone those things which we ought to have done. And we have done those things we ought not to have done and there is no health in us' had become all too familiar.

She endeavoured to bring to the front of her mind those feelings of guilt that had been so dominant in her previous world. Father had said white lies were allowed if they were told to help the feelings of others, but somehow she had always felt it was she who benefited from them.

Since her body had become detached from her mind, her brain cells, confined within the cramped cavity of her skull, were sparring for head space. There were millions of them, far outnumbering the myriad of stars in the galaxies that were now her near neighbours. They had the universe for their playground whereas her cells were contained in that invisible, unattractive grey tissue, each one trying, fighting its own corner – good and evil, them and us, memory and imagination. It was time to release them and see where space took them.

Observa had gleaned her knowledge about brain cells when she couldn't sleep and had turned on the telly in the middle of the night and watched an Open University programme. Then her mind and body were as one, and her body had put a brake on things, been an arbitrator, lessened the misjudgements.

Totally irrelevant thoughts were flooding in and, once there, refusing to leave. They hummed a tune she did not particularly like. Even detached from her body, her mind (or was it her soul?) was having problems thinking straight. Perhaps the mind was the halfway house between body and soul, and your Maker gave you a little time to adjust.

> O young Lochinvar is come out of the west,
> Through all the wide Border his steed was the best;
> And save his good broadsword he weapons had none,

He rode all unarm'd, and he rode all alone.
So faithful in love, and so dauntless in war,
There never was knight like the young Lochinvar.

There were other verses that she could not remember, though she did recall that the poem had a happy ending. It mentioned Netherby Hall, in the ballroom of which she had danced in her youth, and the Solway that was so familiar from happy seaside holidays at Allonby, holding Father's hand as they paddled and looked for shells, his trousers rolled up to just under his knees, her dress tucked into her knickers. The soothing swish of shallow wavelets disguised the sewage that floated by unrecognised.

Her brain had escaped dementia and, unshackled from its physical self, was enjoying its freedom. She had imagined – and hoped – that once she became completely detached and was no longer hovering in sight of her remains, physical anxiety would no longer exist. The heart palpitations and nausea would cease, out of sight, out of mind, now that her mind was free to roam and do its own thing.

It was as though old age had tossed a coin: heads you keep your marbles and land up in a wheelchair; tails you lose them and have to be restrained for fear of wandering off. Had her head overruled her body, or was it the other way around?

*

Was there anything so important that it needed atoning

for immediately? Had petty misjudgements and mistakes changed people's opinion of her, or was she being over-sensitive?

Perhaps she would run into good old Aunt Margaret and have a chance to say sorry...

Dear Aunt M, the recipient of childish pranks and unkind whisperings behind her back, a 'maiden aunt', though she was only 'maiden' because any possible mates had been slaughtered in the war to end all wars.

She had been one of the two million women of her generation destined to spinsterhood and to be the butt of music-hall jokes back in the day when most families had a maiden aunt. Now Observa wished she had resisted joining in the giggles and prayed that her aunt had been oblivious to them. As children, they had made fun of her even before they reached her small bungalow. Why hadn't Mother stopped them?

It had all started with Aunt M's fruit cake, lovingly baked for the arrival of her nephews and nieces on their compulsory Sunday afternoon visit to show family solidarity. Tea had started with cucumber sandwiches, then the famous words that ever after became apocryphal within the family: 'Now, darlings, you must have some of Aunt Margaret's special fruit cake. I made it specially for you.'

And so she had and it was indeed special; even visibly it was a non-starter. Burnt black and over-cooked, it was inedible.

Mother had caught their eyes and suggested that, as it was a lovely day, would Aunt M mind if they took their cake into the garden and ate it outside? As children they had never looked beyond the palatable; had they taken the trouble to get to know Aunt M, later in life they would have had the guidance and friendship of a truly remarkable person.

Thank God she had died when she did and did not have to witness what mankind had made of itself in the twenty-first century.

As the only niece, Observa had inherited her aunt's papers. Hidden among them, she had found a black-and-white photo of a boy, perhaps nine or ten, with blond wavy hair and a happy, smiling face. The inscription was *Will at Budleigh Salterton 1907*, then scribbled in a different hand, *Killed on the Somme 1917, grave unknown*. Father had told Observa that Aunt M's hair had turned virgin white overnight when she had heard of Will's death.

Now she saw Aunt M's impenetrable smile, her face a mirror that reflected her genuine love of everyone. She had reached her solitary old age with dignity and grace, and her beauty had never faded; the lines on her face were so entrenched that even though she may not have been smiling she looked as though she always was. Her deportment was faultless even in her nineties.

What was it she used to say? 'Don't slouch, dear. Sit up straight and always stand upright, it's good for the heart and lungs.' Aunt M had served as a nurse during World War 1, then trained as a physiotherapist; she'd had a thriving, lucrative practice in Hastings holding remedial classes for the pupils of the numerous private preparatory schools that littered the south coast in those days. She had jokingly told Observa that she had a very adequate pension due to the flat feet of the children of indulgent parents.

At the end of Aunt M's life Observa had tried to make amends for her childish insensitivity and take responsibility for Father's only sister. There had been a call from neighbours: her aunt had not been seen for thirty-six hours and they thought she should know. Aunt M had been found slumped on the floor in the corner of the kitchen wrapped in an old rug; how long she had been there, no one knew.

Guilt set in; this would be Observa's final chance to turn attrition into contrition, but it would have to be *meant*, worked at. You couldn't just click a switch to make amends.

After two weeks in hospital recovering from pneumonia, Aunt M had been keen to get home but it was obvious that, at ninety-four, she could no longer look after herself. A suitable care home must be located and inspected; it would not be easy for she had high standards, and her possessions were few but beautiful. She had what her generation had called 'taste', and the bottom drawer of her Georgian bow-fronted chest of drawers still held flowered boxes from Liberty's and Debenhams with their tissue paper intact.

The first plan was to find somewhere near Aunt M's present home where her friends could visit. Observa had spent many hours and gallons of petrol looking for somewhere she felt her aunt would be happy. It had been a depressing experience: Aunt M would not take kindly to eating communally off bare Formica tables and Tupperware plates.

It was a stroke of luck that Observa had remembered something Mother had said about a friend's friend who had found a place by the sea in the south of the county, roughly 150 miles away, a home from home where the friend had been happy.

She had set aside a whole day to go and do a recce. It was a beautiful house set on a hill in its own grounds overlooking the sea with breathtaking views. It was a good start.

She was greeted at the front door with its Georgian portico by someone who smiled. A huge log fire was burning, its warmth permeated an area that contained six or seven dining tables, places set with the correct cutlery for two or four guests. Long white tablecloths reached the floor and the napkins were linen, some contained in a personal napkin ring and others in the shape of a swan. It was hardly necessary to look at the bedroom; she had known immediately that this was the place for Aunt M.

And so it had proved. Aunt M was taken there by subterfuge, told that she was going on a little holiday – it was white-lie time again. But she had spent three contented years there. She was given the responsibility of watering the flower arrangements, and in her final year had convinced herself – and most of the residents – that she owned the house and they were her guests. The staff went along with it because everyone seemed happy.

On Observa's fortnightly visits, Aunt M had greeted her with the words, 'Come and meet my friend So-and-

So. She's staying with me for the weekend. I have put her in the blue/green/pink room.'

Throughout her life, Aunt M had accepted responsibility. If you did the wrong thing, you shouldered the blame; there were no human rights' laws to let you off the hook. Now the culture was to find someone else to blame; you no longer needed to get your facts straight, just Tweet away and say what you liked. Trusted adages had been swept away; 'sticks and stones may break my bones but words can never hurt me' had been turned on its head. Lies that remained unchallenged quickly became the truth.

✳

Despite the popular belief that you saw your whole life pass by when your soul left your body, it felt nothing like that. Death appears to descend like some God-sent heavenly crusher that compacted your life, leaving your soul to float free. Observa hoped it would stay like that and that she would not land up in limbo.

Earth and its travails were still preying on her mind; she worried about the children, grandchildren and great-grandchildren and that destroyed the promised 'peace of God which passeth all understanding'.

Had words in Heaven changed their meaning, as they had on earth? She had been chuffed when, at sixteen, she had passed her school certificate with a credit in English, but the words she had used in her essay on happiness were now forbidden. The truth of God's word had been made invalid: trivialised and satirised.

It might be difficult to get the measure of life after death, and adopting a non-lifestyle might not be easy. Even when she'd had a body to support her, she could not master new technology or the new language that went with it. Apps and podcasts had proved more challenging than French irregular verbs; she had floundered in the sea of 'could do better' and been left behind in that brave new world.

There were a few free spirits still out there courageous enough to speak the truth, and her old age had brought them to her door. There was the postman, a migrant who loved his job in all weathers, stayed for a chat and talked about freedom and ignored the tachograph in his van. And that poor man, Sam, who had delivered the oil until the activists got to him and he took his own life. Charming university friends of her grandchildren used to pop in to see her from time to time. No longer allowed open discussion in their university debating societies, they sat at her kitchen table like members of the French Resistance and kept their minds afloat.

Between her four walls, they had cracked blasphemous jokes about the new god of personal sexuality. They had assured her that the Trans-Pennine Railway was being renamed because passengers were no longer certain whether they were north, south, east or west bound. She had always kept a supply of real ale in the fridge for them and cooked them impromptu meals until the supplies ran out.

✳

There was a strong presence behind her and she knew instantly that it was Aunt M. Could it be that in order to connect to those who had gone before, all you had to do was to think of the person and they would appear? 'Appear' was the wrong word – 'awareness' was more accurate – but the certainty that they were with you was all that was needed

Perhaps she still carried an earthly scent as all mammals did to keep their families united; maybe it was something programmed into you at birth to attract you to your own kith and kin.

She was aware of the electricity within her own body. How many times, whilst undressing on a frosty night, had her vest crackled when she had pulled it over her head? Sometimes sparks had been visible. Recently, when grabbing her Zimmer in the dark, her hand had experienced a short, sharp shock, so anything was possible.

All those years of doubt. She should have tried harder at joking her way through life, been the life and soul of the party. She had tried it once in her youth, acting the giddy goat, but she had not got away with it. She was unsure what impression she had made, unsure whether her words had caused amusement or embarrassment, and she had quickly reverted to her role as wallflower. Mother would have described such behaviour in a daughter as unbecoming; carrying on in such a way was unseemly.

Others had almost got away with it. There was that politician way back, untidily dressed, with his unkempt blond hair and his shirt hanging out. He had considered himself an eccentric, a trait once admired by the

British. But 'mad dogs and Englishmen' were no longer fashionable and it was too late for him to learn new ropes.

She needed to say goodbye to the crumpled heap on the ground and the creased mustard trousers and move on, but her mind was reluctant because she hadn't really dealt with atonement and it was needed closer to home. Regret was still gnawing away at her, too.

She had betrayed her own mother. It had seemed expedient at the time to keep the peace, to make her own life more bearable and to save her marriage, which even then she knew was not a marriage worth saving. She had quickly turned Judas; that is what came of trying to please too many people.

When Father had died, Mother had seemed to imagine that she was going to start a new life at eighty-five and do all the things she had always wanted to do. She had immediately sold the family home and purchased a property with an old schoolfriend of the same age. The venture was destined for disaster from the start; old schoolfriends changed over the years, and by the time they were in their eighties they were inclined to be set in their ways. Even the things Mother had said about this childhood friendship should have been a red flag.

'She was rather spoilt as a child,' Mother had commented, which was ironic considering she herself was pretty immovable over certain things. They should have foreseen trouble.

It had only taken six months for acrimony to build and that telephone conversation to take place when Observa delivered those fatal words so flippantly: 'You can always come and live with us.' And so, two weeks later Mother had, with a promise to Hugh that it would be a temporary arrangement.

She was put in the spare room with its pretty, pink, out-of-date Laura Ashley wallpaper and a lovely view over the garden. Things had gone moderately smoothly for five weeks until Hugh started asking when Mother was leaving.

Observa had countered that with, 'We must be hospitable. Think of all the times we were welcomed into her home,' but her words had no effect. She had pointed out how much she enjoyed having her mother live with them, although that was another white lie.

It had become exhausting. Eventually she had insisted that Mother stay in bed in the mornings to lessen the tensions at the breakfast table.

The climax came midsummer when the garden was looking its best. It was an excellent year for roses, and Hugh was looking forward to entering three blooms in the horticultural section of the local agricultural show. Mother had strict instructions not to touch the roses, but she had cut three blooms and come into the kitchen for a glass jar in which to put them to take up to her bedroom. Whether she did it on purpose, or old age had made her forgetful, or she'd thought she was still living in her own domain, it was the straw that broke the camel's back. From resentful tolerance, outright war was declared.

✳

Looking down, Observa saw that bramble tendrils were already curling themselves maliciously around her hands and wrists, their tiny harpoon thorns penetrating her skin. They would soon smother the tiny green sprouts of fescues that were just visible, pushing their way between the fingers of her outstretched hands as they sensed the presence of the nutrients that would be released when her body returned to dust.

What a relief that her body had become detached from her mind. It was finally free to do its own thing, no longer bound to obey, no longer obliged to give conjugal rights and carry around the demands of age.

She had always known that her body was not much good at physical challenges and meeting demands. She was well aware that, had she been faced with imprisonment, deprivation and any of the growing number of atrocities the human race inflicted upon itself, her body would not have lasted a week. Her mind might have made it as many of those of her generation had done; they had appeared on the telly from time to time, telling their tales of survival in breathless, cracked voices, giving warnings that were never listened to. Their minds had been firmly rooted; who had commented that trees and plants have roots but man has only legs, and those have been his downfall? They had made him discontented with his own green grass and led him to search for pastures new.

*

She had put off discussing Mother's future until they were in the car together, trying to choose her words carefully so as not to upset and hurt.

Although her mother had not been the most affectionate, she had been a good parent. She had been an educator, for she had inherited her own father's love of language and she'd made up silly poems and limericks that, to the embarrassment of her family, she was inclined to recite in the company of strangers. She'd had a sense of fun, something Observa's husband had never possessed.

'Mum, darling, we're going to have to think again about your future. I think you'd be much happier in one of those little flats with someone to keep half an eye on you and cook your meals.'

White lies again; she had been doing the same as she had done to Aunt M.

The response had been swift; Mother had not made things easy. 'I am far too old to start again.' But in the end she had, and Observa's sense of guilt and betrayal had become overwhelming.

But with the fortitude of her generation Mother had adapted, just as Aunt M had done. She had ruled the roost and, when the drains in the old people's home became blocked and a plumber could not be found, she had taken things into her own hands. Using the large soup ladle from the kitchen, she had removed the drain cover, got down on her hands and knees and swiftly unblocked it as she made a comment about British workmen.

✳

The crows had already taken her eyes and were pecking at her mouth. She remembered long ago racing across the fields at lambing time, her lungs bursting, to get to a ewe that was giving birth. She had needed to foil the crows that were sitting on the drystone wall awaiting the emergence of the lamb's head, yellow with birth fluid.

The crows had descended quickly and plucked an eye from its socket then squabbled over the second one, even though the lamb's body was still not birthed.

A fox cautiously approached Observa's body then tentatively snatched at and pulled off an ear. It stood back before attempting more, making sure it was not outnumbered by the crows for there was strength in numbers and they would quickly turn on him.

She saw that it was an old dog fox, emaciated and mange ridden, its mask and brush devoid of hair, an urban fox out of its comfort zone.

Chapter 5

The time had come to explore her new world and to try and find Father. She would take her mind on a spiritual pub crawl, revisit and look down upon all those hostelries, the egalitarian watering holes of her youth where the craic was good and the lord of the manor bought the poacher a flagon of ale. Were they still there with their familiar names – The Stag Inn, The Dog and Duck, The Fox and Hounds, The Grey Goat?

Observa knew that the Yanwath Yat had been renamed the Yanwath Gate; perhaps its latest owners had been unsure of the rural vernacular. Rumour had it that Reuben, the elderly village sage who for a decade had occupied his special reserved corner of the bar near the open fire, had no longer felt welcome; his unkempt appearance, slight whiff and dialect ramblings had disturbed the new clientele.

Did The Fish Inn still hold its position on the isthmus between Buttermere and Crummock, or had it been renamed and revamped to please an urban population and the tourist industry? Had its leather armchairs, into which she had sunk with her first gin and orange, been replaced by hard, chromium bar stools, their origins mined from beneath the primal forests of the Bushveld?

There was profit to be made, so all was well with the world – and there was always artificial intelligence to look forward to. Thank goodness she no longer was part of it – although she would have appreciated an extension of her youth and more time to visit all those exciting, unspoilt places that the young now went to as a rite of passage, ticking them off the list, all sense of adventure evaporated.

She would like to have been allowed to hover over them and take a peek, but she was starting to understand the rules of the afterlife. You were only allowed to reconnect with, or be aware of, places you had visited during your life.

She must not assume that Mother would be with Father, should she find him. In the flesh they had not been seen as a particularly clinging couple, and she suspected that they had only got together to procreate; they were certainly not Dante and Beatrice.

Observa was well aware of couples among her friends who never spoke to one another but appeared perfectly happy within their marriage. They were probably now seeking their own like minds, those whose minds theirs had briefly encountered but never taken up with nor acted upon.

The only evidence of family togetherness had been that lovely photo, a black-and-white snapshot taken by a visitor. Observa had put it to one side when going through the drawers full of photos of unknown people in readiness for the bin and her own departure, and she had placed it on the smaller 'to keep' pile.

Months later she had looked for it, just to reassure herself that her family had once existed and the image she carried in her head was the correct one.

She thought of those art-appreciation classes at school when you were shown a well-known painting and invited to describe what you believed was happening. She had been good at that, got an A-star. Now, because of her untidiness and lack of concentration and her tendency to muddle through life and do five things at once, she had put the photograph in the wrong pile and it was lost forever.

No one would ever bear witness that they had once been a family; the only evidence was in her mind and could not be transferred. There it would remain, undiscovered, etched into her brain.

In the photograph, Father was on the back row dressed as she always remembered him with his stained, soft brown trilby at a rakish angle, pipe in mouth, a tall, slight figure wearing his everyday uniform of tweed jacket and plus-fours, tie and shirt, knee-length thick woollen socks and shiny-clean brown brogues. He always polished his own shoes, including the sole between the heel and toecap. The twelve-bore was slung nonchalantly over his right arm and his left arm was around Mother's waist. He had always been contented with his lot.

Mother was wearing a flowered cotton dress; her thinness was evident, and her fashionable lack of breasts and bobbed hair dated the picture to the late 1920s. She was looking straight ahead and her hands were resting on Observa's shoulders.

Observa wished she could remember that day because they all looked happy, though she did recall hating her outfit. She appeared to have been dressed up for an occasion in that special dress of shantung, the turquoise and light-blue material delivered from Liberty's to be made up by the village seamstress around her protesting body. The matching hair ribbon controlled her annoying calf lick.

She recalled being told how grateful she should be to have a dress made specially from pongee, a rough wild silk from the north-east region of China. Her white ankle socks were encased in black-leather pumps with criss-cross elastic to keep them in place.

How she had hated dressing up for other people, made to be someone she didn't want to be; it was so unlike putting on the dressing-up clothes in the nursery ottoman that allowed you to be whoever you desired.

She wished she could have been portrayed in the photo like her two elder brothers: in welly boots with their four-tens slung under their right arms, off for a day's rough shooting with Father. They must only have been about nine and eleven, but they were already good marksmen; their apprenticeship had been strict and they were true countrymen with the responsibility of carrying a gun drilled into them as a rite of passage. They could whistle up rats and dispatch them with an accurately placed bullet.

Her little brother was sitting on the grass, his arm around Jem, Father's golden retriever. The photo was not quite in focus and the familiar background had a dreamlike, hazy quality; it could have been an illustration in a child's book of fairy tales. The tulip tree was only half visible, its dark flowers in bloom, standing proud in the middle of the side lawn where it had been planted by a maternal great-grandfather many decades ago.

In the far distance was the Wet Hen, so christened by her siblings for its resemblance to one. It was a giant deodar cedar that had started life as a sapling on the lower slopes of the Himalayas, where it had absorbed a certain spirituality. Its branches had been decimated by centuries of gales and the remaining ones, where the nightjars roosted, hung like damp feathers. Taller than other trees and visible for miles around, it stood sentinel where the main lawn ran parallel to the road.

That was the landmark they spotted excitedly as they returned home from the misery of boarding school in the safety of the old Rover that smelt of damp dog. Half a mile from home they would start screaming, 'The Wet Hen! The Wet Hen! The Wet Hen!' as it came into sight.

Now, a century later, how would those who held sway see the picture? What interpretation or misinterpretation would they put on it? Guns had been demonised in urban minds by tut-tutting media celebs and the vociferous clever-clever-clever young who knew it all. They could tell the difference between TikTok and Twitter but not between a black and a brown rat as they donned their balaclavas to stir up hatred against country folk.

Nothing in life had been as it seemed. Humankind had been taken in, bewitched by image, thought suffocating beneath the giant throw of advertising. Lemming-like, people had flung themselves in a mad rush over the cliff of consumerism into the seething destructive sea of greed that lay below.

She and Father had refused to become slaves to the system because they understood instinctively that the system had got it wrong. But it was all very well repeating 'Build not treasures upon earth where rust and dust corrupt and thieves break in and steal' when it was happening all around and no one was listening.

She had binned old family photos unthinkingly and carelessly, casually thrown them into the waste-paper basket, and now the images were no longer there for future generations to ponder over. How easy it had been to make a mistake; in tidying out her life, she had thrown away the irreplaceable.

Although she could recreate it in her memory, her past would remain unseen to others unless – unless there was still a way for it to be discovered…

That other small, crumpled sepia snapshot had escaped her impetuosity and was still in the house somewhere; would it ever be found or understood? She was unsure whether anyone had survived to find it because there had been no signs of human life for some time.

That photograph, a faded picture of a blond-haired little boy wearing a Christopher Robin smock, would be of no interest to those intent on survival. Who would care that he had been an only child, his mind trained for leadership, duty and honour at Rugby School, then blown to bits on the Western Front, his grave unknown.

Forgotten. Every generation carried its own self-created burden of guilt and conflict. Her generation had been fortunate; they had lived through wars in which their opponents had been visible. The enemy today had arrived stealthily, been made welcome in homes as it snaked its way in under cover of the latest technology, a tangle of wires insulated by a non-biodegradable protective covering that offered an apple.

Unable to differentiate between good and evil, homo sapiens had been bewitched by their own ingenuity and acted as midwives at the birth of its wireless offspring. Jubilation had welcomed its birth; sponsors, financiers and entrepreneurs in their Towers of Babel had held parties. It had been baptised and given the name ARTIFICIAL INTELLIGENCE.

Not everyone was happy to welcome this new Messiah, but the naysayers had been slow to find their voices.

At what stage in life's cycle was man no longer made flesh? The brain was obviously part of flesh, and she'd been quite happy to leave it behind, but what about the mind that she felt was now in charge and calling the tune? Perhaps the mind was the halfway house to the ultimate place where worries no longer existed – but at what stage did the soul finally take over? Was it up to her to make the transition and press some button? She was anxious that if she got it wrong she might elbow the stars from their orbit like some man-made satellite.

Unlike her brothers, who had managed to ignore it, she

had been aware of the inevitability of death from an early age. At the age of six it had come to her in a flash.

She had been in the boys' bedroom, forbidden territory, standing by the door on the uneven old floorboards that creaked underfoot. Through the open window, listening to the boys playing their version of cricket in the garden, she had realised that one day her parents would be gone. How would she manage without them?

✻

The breakdown had started slowly. The churches were the first to go, their messages misunderstood, the ten commandments – those few words and signposts to happiness – cast aside and binned like the cooking instructions on a prepacked joint of meat. The words of the new prophets were written on a subway train, and those that had stirred the souls of earlier generations were scorned and pilloried.

Dog started to eat dog, and people learned how to snarl online at one another. Lies left unchallenged were quickly accepted as the truth. The grim reaper stood outside the door and tent flap of every home. The rich man in his castle, the poor man at his gate; levelling up was really happening. Parents could no longer reassure their children with 'count your blessings' or 'think of those worse off than yourself'. Everyone was in the same boat and Noah's ark was no longer seaworthy.

✻

Once upon a time dying was easy: you just popped your clogs and hoped there was still someone out there prepared to bury or cremate you. Some people made a good living out of doing that. Observa remembered all those reassuring, persuasive ads depicting a balmy spring day with a butterfly fluttering, tempting you to participate in prepaid arrangements.

That emotional insurance scam for clever forward planning was meant to prevent your children having any hassle when the time came. The companies pocketed the premiums; there was nothing in the small print to warn you that there might be no one left to honour the agreement.

Father used to say, 'Stay away from funerals. They are death traps for the elderly.' Statistics had shown that to be true; a high percentage of the elderly caught pneumonia by standing around open graves trying to say the right thing. There had been that *Insight* programme about it on the telly.

She was hearing Father's thoughts again, so he must be in the vicinity. If she concentrated on him really hard, he would come to her, guide her as he had done in life, soothe her anxieties and wash her wounds.

Then it struck her that perhaps it needed to be the other way round. Perhaps in the afterlife things were reversed and she must be the guide and seek *him* out, forget her own trivial inadequacies and try and deal with his, the moments of self-doubt that he had carried throughout his life but hidden from her.

It was time for her to help him; that was what atonement meant.

Chapter 6

Had Observa imagined that tap on her shoulder? Someone was trying to make contact and, just as an amputee feels an itch on a limb long after it has gone, her body had transferred its awareness to her mind.

It was not the souls of others that she must seek but her own. In life she had never found herself, but now was her chance; free from the burden of earthly duties and responsibilities, she might discover what sort of person she really was – but that would require feedback. Part of her wanted to succeed, be lauded for her achievements; the other part, which had acquired the upper hand in life, had tried to hide and had despised exposure.

Now she had no desire to become one of those mythical souls who aimlessly wandered the heavens searching for God-only-knew what – she'd had too much of that on Earth. If she could go back to a time when she was really happy, perhaps it would be possible to redress the balance, relive shared good times, not those fleeting moments of glorious bliss that some people thought were worth an age without a name, but those rare moments of being content with your lot.

Observa would take one more trip to bid farewell to her body, make the final break with that with which she had been intimate for almost a century.

She was curious to see what time had done to it as it lay there lifeless. She had been alarmed by the speed of her decomposition: the flesh on her face had disappeared, gnawed at until her skull and jaw bones had been exposed; bluebottles were crawling inquisitively into her eye sockets; her teeth, which in their final years had caused her so much hidden grief, coupled with a good deal of expense and wounded vanity, were fully visible.

Observa looked at the bluebottles more closely, for they no longer struck her as unpleasant. During her long days of loneliness in the house she had been pleased to have their company; they were something animate, survivors like herself, satiated by the abundance of carrion that assured their future. Swarms of them had sought what little warmth there was in her home during times of bitter cold and she had adapted well to their presence, just as she had to the rats that were Extinction Rebellion's success story.

Once, she had considered all flies to be a nuisance and the kitchen cupboard was full of dried-up sprays that had guaranteed their demise. Now, with time on her hands, Observa started to observe them more closely. There was one in particular, a blowfly for whom she had gained respect, and she admired the delicacy of its wings and its fluorescent beauty. It was larger than the others and she recognised it: its genus was Calliphora Vomitori.

Knowledge gained during her time as PA to the director of the Commonwealth Institute of Entomology was paying off. What had been her boss's name? She couldn't remember, it was not filed correctly in the appropriate brain cell, but she remembered *him*: a kindly, brilliant but eccentric man. She had been no good at filing and he had chastised her good humouredly.

Oh, and all those charming field officers from Commonwealth countries with whom Observa had flirted when they visited London biannually to pool their research and knowledge at conferences. Lovely Dr Kapur from Madras: Observa had persuaded him to join her Scottish dancing group and endeavoured to teach him the intricacies of the eightsome reel. He had been bemused but polite; happier with the more restrained, mellow sounds of the sitar, he had tried to adapt to the bagpipes with little success. However, his paper on the control of mosquitoes as part of the search for a cure for malaria had been widely praised and printed in *The Lancet*.

Although uncertain of the gender of her new acquaintance the blowfly, Observa had named him Fred; only later would she rechristen him Einstein when it became clear just how intelligent he was. He had learned to avoid the flypaper that had entrapped so many of his friends and relatives; when she had first become aware of him, he was examining a dirty tea towel with a faded imprint of Fountains Abbey on it.

They had things in common: she had caught his eye and he was looking at her, summing her up. If only he could communicate, he could tell her whether the rumours had been true about Asian hornets swarming across the Channel, killing the native population of honey bees and taking their mutilated bodies back to their nests to feed to their young.

Homo sapiens had lost the ability to stop them, and urban man had been forced to take refuge. To escape the swarms of insects, people had sought the sanctuary of their homes, glass tower blocks that had won architectural awards for easy living. But, as temperatures rose and the power supply failed, they were trapped. Those glass-walled edifices, those grand designs lauded as 'living at its best', had become death traps. Spectators watched as the occupants were slowly incinerated, cremated before their eyes as they scratched at the windows, their screams unheard through the soundproof, shatterproof glass.

Never again would Observa complain about the inconvenience and expense of living in a listed building with its crumbling sandstone and ill-fitting sash windows, where rats scampered in the rubble cavities of its three-feet-thick stone walls that gave protection from the intense heat.

She welcomed the rats' presence and the sound of them at night when she couldn't sleep because she no longer had to worry that they might be eating through an electricity cable since all the cables were lifeless. Observa suspected that the rats had created a maternity ward underneath the floor of the linen cupboard, having remembered its past warmth where their forebears had gone to die and give succour to maggots.

Had she still been attached to her body, it would be recoiling at the memory of maggots and shivering at the recall of her hand up the backside of a sheep as she used her fingers to scrape away the grubs before they had a chance to devour their host alive.

Of course she knew that all those creepy-crawlies had as much right to be on the planet as she did and, given the chance and left alone, would probably make a success of it. Who was it who had written 'Big fleas have little fleas upon their backs to bite 'em and those fleas have lesser fleas' and so on ad infinitum? She had a feeling it was Jonathan Swift.

Humans were the only species hell-bent on destroying themselves and they'd made a pretty good job of it.

In order to retain her sanity, she had found it necessary to go outside, to lift her face to the burning sun for just a minute and watch the clouds that were as timeless and beautiful as ever. No longer did the vapour trail of planes dissect the sun's rays; they were long gone.

Man's belief in his own clever-cleverness had been exposed. He had become absorbed in his own arrogance and dismissed the idea that out there may be a power greater than himself. He had discarded the wisdom of his forbears.

Planes had started falling from the skies – metal fatigue, they had called it.

✳

Nature had become Observa's diary and it set the pace:

years, months, weeks, days, hours, minutes. Seconds no longer had any meaning.

When the heat was not too intense and the leaves were on the turn, Observa sat outside in the old wicker garden chair counting the seconds of exposure for exactly one minute, happy to share the space with insects that had made it their home and in the company of butterflies. Fresh from pupating, they rested on the whitewashed walls of the house, gently opening and closing their wings to dry them.

The butterflies had adapted well to the soaring temperatures; sometimes they rested on her knee, attracted by the yellow of her moleskins. Admirals and Peacocks, so beautiful; she had tried to differentiate between the large and small Tortoiseshells – one had three black spots the other four – but she could never remember which was which.

She had to be careful not to doze off because sometimes the chair became her magic carpet; as well as carrying her to Dreamland, it could take her back to places she had no wish to revisit. Also, she had to keep reminding herself that the sun was no longer her friend.

From time to time she returned to the gardens of her youth. She knew a bank whereon the wild thyme blows, where oxlip and the nodding violet grows, and the eglantine had been wonderful that last spring, filling the hedgerows with colour and scent and hearts with joy…

If you were to believe in Shakespeare, as Observa always had, where were the promised angels to sing her to her rest? Letting go was proving to be more difficult than she had imagined.

✳

Someone had just taken hold of her hand; the fingers were familiar, soft and warm with a scent of lavender water. Observa looked up expecting to see angels but recognised her grandmother.

Suddenly she was back in her childhood home, standing outside a bedroom that had been turned into a sickroom when Granny had come to live and die with them.

The brusque district nurse emerged saying, 'Your grandmother has gone to the other side. You may go in and say goodbye.' What did she mean 'gone to the other side'? Granny was still on her usual side of the big double bed.

Observa had tried to lean over to give her a kiss but even on tiptoe she couldn't reach, so she had kissed her cold hand and said, 'Goodnight, Granny.'

Now they were standing holding hands in the graveyard of an isolated rural church, a church in miniature, its Norman tower dwarfed by the ancient yew trees that surrounded it. Granny was saying, 'So sad, so sad. Those poor people.'

Observa thought she was talking about the dead people lying beneath the gravestones but she wasn't: she was talking about the living.

She tried to sort out the time scale: if she really was with Granny, it must be the 1930s – and then she knew why she was there again. If her memory served her right, Father would be somewhere around.

She widened her gaze and saw once again the valley of Mardale. She remembered Granny saying, "They have promised that the church will be demolished before it is drowned and the stones used to build another church on higher ground.'

It had been a broken promise: the stones had been used to build the turreted draw tower that had stuck out of the lake and become a tourist attraction. The stonemasons, sensing the sanctity of the stones, queried what they were being used for, but it had been a question of cost and sanctity hadn't come into it.

The Haweswater dam and the flooding of Mardale had been a talking point among adults for many months, a topic of conversation at dinner parties where guests spoke of 'drowning Paradise to flush the bloody loos of Manchester' and suggested writing to their MP to make him 'earn his Westminster money'. In The Dun Bull Inn, also soon to be under water, voices were raised about 'stealing our land to swill the bloody privvies of townsfolk' as final pints were drawn and downed resignedly.

Observa had been too young to fully understand, though Father had insisted that she was not. 'It is important to understand at an early age the sacrifices we all have to make for the common good.' He had become involved professionally, something to do with compensation.

She and Granny had walked back over the narrow chapel bridge to find him sitting in the kitchen of Goosemire farmhouse savouring strong tea out of an enamel mug and homemade scones straight from the oven of the black-leaded cast-iron range that dominated the room, its warmth soon to be quenched forever.

Observa had been thinking about the rabbits. 'What will happen to the baby rabbits? Will they drown in their nests, Granny?' she had asked.

'It's not like filling a bath, darling. The water trickles in slowly so they will have plenty of time to reach higher ground. Their natural instincts will warn them of danger.'

Father had added, almost under his breath, 'I fear mankind may have lost his natural instincts.'

Observa had an ambivalent relationship with rabbits. Her days of ferreting with her brothers had made her conscious of the labyrinth of underground passages and boltholes that they called home. It was not a good thing to over-sentimentalise animals, particularly if you enjoyed eating them; it was important to see their negative attributes before becoming mawkish about them.

She remembered the itching that followed after she had carried newly caught rabbits into the kitchen of her childhood home to be dealt with by the cook. The fleas, like rats deserting a sinking ship, had transferred their allegiance to her and her arms had been covered in bites; they had even got into her knickers before Mother could apply Dettol.

Now Observa could see every detail of the farm kitchen as though she were still there. With hindsight, that which she had taken for granted as a child bore significance. As a child she had never got to know her maternal grandmother; she had been too young to appreciate her. Granny had been an ethereal presence who sometimes came to tea, and for whom Observa was made to put on clean clothes and wash her hands. Until she finally came to live with them to die.

Granny was now sitting opposite her in a rocking chair, a reassuring presence. At first glance her clothes appeared unsuited for a day among the hills and country folk, but because of their elegance and the way she moved within them they never looked out of place. They had the simplicity of good taste: jersey-silk softness and muted colours, the Chanel look of emancipation as women broke out of the hard shell of male dominance after the slaughter of the trenches. At least her grandmother's generation had escaped the degradation of man-made fibres. To Observa's childish eyes, the single long string of pearls that reached below Granny's waist looked perfect and complemented her cloche hat.

CHAPTER 7

Mother used to talk about her childhood and her mother a great deal, but as a child Observa had failed to listen. It was a family fable that grandmother had been an orphan at the latter end of the nineteenth century, but that had turned out to be a myth.

Now Observa would have a chance to hear the real story from its protagonist, not imaginative hand-me-downs that had distorted the truth and turned it into a modern-day sob story of an impoverished Irish family seeking a better life in New Zealand and leaving their youngest child behind. The reality had been very different, and here was her grandmother in another world putting things straight.

Observa knew of her family's connections with the Friends' movement; there were great uncles who were Quakers and she'd always had a vague awareness of them, together with other hearsay. There were notes written in pencil on old family papers waiting to be gone through and collated; she had never got round to it and that deepened the sea of guilt in which she now swam.

Heaven alone knew what had happened to them.

She must try to accept that nothing mattered any more. Her mind was now free to imagine whatever it liked; there was no one, no thing, no functioning digital gadget that could verify anything.

However, there were still books littering houses, half read. Towards the end, Observa had rummaged through her bookcases despite her failing sight. She had been saddened and ashamed by the state into which she had allowed the books to fall. She had allowed neglect to damage them, and it reminded her of a time when she would have been upset to find moths among her woollies.

She had far outlived her last pair of glasses and the lenses had been buckled by the intense, unfiltered rays of the sun. Even so, she had hoped to keep her sight for a little longer.

For the past months, just keeping going had been her priority and she really hadn't taken much notice of what was happening to her books. She hoped the sweltering dry heat had not tempted termites to leave their desert home and move north.

Observa remembered her brother-in-law, a lover of literature and a military man, who had been seconded to the Middle East during the Suez fiasco. He'd told her how he'd had to leave Egypt in a hurry. His books were too heavy to take on the plane so they were left at the dock in Port Said to be forwarded to the UK when transport became available. Red termites had found the books first. The insurance company decreed that the policy covered all termites – with the exclusion of red ones.

Now insurance was also a thing of the past.

When she had opened the glass-fronted bookcase, the first title to catch her eye among the riff raff of popular novels of their day was a stout, leather-bound King James's Holy Bible, the edge of each fragile, tissue-thin page still gold leafed. Next to it was a copy of *All Passion Spent* by Vita Sackville-West.

As Observa pulled it out, it had crumbled to dust in her hand. The termites had long since gone but they had left their calling cards of husks as they destroyed the words on the page.

Strangely, the Bible was still intact.

What had made her forbears decide to up stumps and relocate to New Zealand in the 1880s? Observa would never know. By all accounts they were comfortably off; in her youth, her grandmother had been privately educated at home. Her parents had been pillars of the community – but there were other facts that were indisputable.

A week before the family was due to sail Grandmother, who was in her early teens, had contracted typhoid fever. With the family home sold and passages booked, it was decided that she should be left behind and nursed back to health by an aunt. The intention was that she would be reunited at a later date with her parents and brother David in New Zealand.

Granny never saw her close family again. She recovered fully and remained under the loving guardianship of her aunt and her kindly, well-to-do Quaker uncle, a certain Josiah Newman of Bucklands, Wiltshire who had made his fortune in the grocery trade.

His actual existence was confirmed by a silver Georgian teapot known in the family as the Newman Teapot that had been handed down the distaff line. Observa had once warmed her hands upon it, stroked its slender spout and held its ivory handle. It had ended up with Observa's granddaughter; its value misunderstood, it had been placed in the dark tomb of a bank vault, its history and message of love silenced.

Grandmother had decided not to risk New Zealand, a wise decision because Josiah had lavished on his wife's niece all the love and attention and wisdom he had given to his own daughters. His thirst for knowledge had persuaded him that his daughters should be educated as thoroughly as if they were sons, and Granny had joined them as a boarder at a ladies' college in Cheltenham. The school had been ahead of its time, though in the end Granny's fate had been that of so many women of her generation: early nuptials and motherhood.

Future researchers would define her marriage to Observa's grandfather as an arranged one. It had come about when a colleague of Grandfather's had been visiting Josiah Newman's factory to discuss machinery for manufacturing biscuits. He had been invited to Bucklands for dinner that evening and met Granny. He reported, 'Thomas, I have met just the wife for thee.'

This Quaker social networking had borne fruit and, in spite of the age difference, theirs had been a blissfully happy union. Grandmother had never been reunited with her biological family; although there had been half-hearted efforts by future generations to make contact with the Hamptons of New Zealand, of whom there were many, nothing had come of them.

But a lot had come from her education. Her Victorian philanthropic upbringing had rubbed off on her own children, and she had used the classics as a way of speech. She passed that gift on to Observa's mother, who made education fun, always using quotations and making up limericks:

'Conrad, Tennyson and H.G. Wells,
Like E. Nesbit and Maugham, they cast spells.
The magic created,
Though now a bit dated,
Is sheer expertise and it tells!'

A half-written one on the same scrap of paper in Mother's strong, sloping hand read:

For good, for evil and for pleasure,
The power of WORDS NOTHING BEATS…

Those scraps of paper in an old shoe box had been buried in the box room for half a century, to be gone through some time in the future, when it was still possible to believe there would be a future.

There were two in a spidery, almost illegible hand, written when Mother must have been having an inward chuckle as she neared her end:

Michael Philpot, our local optician,
Is also a clever musician.
He was very upset

When his new clarinet
Was smashed by a mathematician.

A disgruntled RC full of malice,
Once stole a most valuable chalice.
I'm sorry to say
He pawned it next day
And ran off with a woman called Alice.

The jottings had become more prolific when Mother entered the care home; she took pleasure in observing the other inmates, which lessened Observa's guilt at having put her there. Mother had found them a source of inspiration.

Social Services Officer Steele
With community matters will deal.
Aids for the old
He'll supply if he's told,
Either fixed or the kind you can wheel.

Mr. Smith has a zimmer like me;
That they are a help, we agree.
Though walking is slow,
We both of us know
They lift pressure off leg and off knee.

Mrs Sattersthwaite, you know,
Is a photography pro.
She has skills you will find
Of a most unique kind
As we found when she gave her slide show.

At home in Flat 10 may be seen
My neighbour called Mrs MacBeen.
She likes to pay Scrabble,
With words she will dabble
With someone who's eager and keen.

And after a visit to a financial adviser and a solicitor…

A financial consultant named Wall,
Several years ago, as I recall,
Gave advice I have found
To be thoroughly sound
And the income Tax reasonably small.

If you're thinking of making a will,
You will need a solicitor's skill. Beneficiaries then
May be satisfied when
You're deceased and he's paying the bill.

Did ladies' colleges still exist? Observa doubted there were any real ladies still around to go to them; women no longer fitted that description and the equality laws had not helped.

She became aware of her grandmother taking her hand and squeezing it as they both thought about the same person who stood as bridge between them.

Although the limericks were undated, Observa could track their progress by the firmness of Mother's handwriting; during the last year of her life it had become a little shaky, though that had been hardly noticeable because her mind was as sharp as ever.

Both Granny and Mother had been allowed to grow old before dementia was invented, a classification that had increased the share price of the pharmaceutical industry.

For her own peace of mind, Observa decided that she would try not to return to any of the misjudgements she had made in her lifetime because there was nothing she could do to right those wrongs. Time changed perception; her thoughts now were different to those she had felt at the time. Redemption was not straightforward; making it through the Pearly Gates was not going to be easy.

CHAPTER 8

Observa had blown away the dust from the bindings of the King James Bible and opened it at random: St. Matthew, 24.

There shall not be left one stone upon another and ye shall hear of wars and rumours of wars, see that ye be not troubled for all these things must come to pass. For nation will rise up against nation and Kingdom against kingdom and there shall be famines and pestilences and earthquakes in divers places, etc, etc, etc.

The prophecies were spot on, but few souls opened the Bible now. It was no longer considered to be a good read; people thought they could do better by absorbing the mindless chatter of social media. Besides, the Bible was too heavy going.

When trying to reassure Observa in times of trouble, Mother had said, 'God will never allow anyone to suffer unless He knows that they can cope with the burden,' but maybe this time God and Mother had both overstepped the mark.

She reread verse six, which seemed rather ambiguous

because Christ seemed to be giving Himself a get-out clause. Could all this human suffering be acceptable in His eyes? Must all these horrors really come to pass?

Perhaps God had fallen out temporarily with His only begotten son. Things like that happened on earth; there were all types of filial bust-ups and even the late King had not been immune.

As on earth as it is in Heaven. Did mankind have to pass through Hell to reach Heaven? That seemed a little unkind, rather like going to the Basilica of St Nicholas in Amsterdam, where you had to run the gauntlet of the red-light district first with its sex shops and semi-clad ladies of all nationalities sitting in upper windows.

How many people during their span on earth managed to put their lives in order? Observa imagined it was very few; like her, most of them had no notion of where their place should be. Almost every country had become a cauldron of malcontents. Once-nourishing cultures and identities had been thrown into the melting pot, replaced by the siren calls of 'the grass is always greener'.

When technology had finally given up the ghost and broken down, it had only taken a second, just the click of a switch. It was too late to turn back.

The art of discourse was already lost, buried beneath decades of too much communication; perception was all that mattered and every person became every other person's enemy. Suspicion and mistrust ruled; trust and truth had been bowdlerised from the vocabulary and the art of understanding sidelined.

Observa remembered well the moment she had lost her virginity on a balmy evening following a May Ball, but she was uncertain exactly when the membrane of trust in society had been severed. That rupture had occurred gradually, and it had overshadowed humanity until almost everyone was engulfed in its sombre dark cloud.

Almost everyone: from time to time, Observa had felt a warm glow because there were still people out there thinking about decency and kindness and trying to make contact.

Right up until the end, Hermione had come to sit at Observa's kitchen table. She had struggled through the debris of a once-thriving community, the smell of death all around her, wary of the feral packs of dogs now giving tongue for blood and revenge.

'It's not all bad!' Hermione had said. 'There are Japanese anemones coming up through the tarmac in the road. I always had problems getting them to take in the garden, especially the white ones. I suspect they need a challenge in life to survive, something to push against.'

Hermione had never been tempted to submit to the burden of marriage; she had been suspicious of the siren call of marital bliss. But she had given birth to the minds of the young pupils in her care, and under her guidance the village school had thrived.

She had emulated the values of the old dame schools in the county, some of which were still standing albeit they had ended their days transformed into second homes and holiday lets. She was a throwback who understood the pleasure of passing on knowledge and watching it being absorbed.

She had retired early, disillusioned when the state took over the curriculum and the three Rs were replaced by targets and inspections, when telling the truth had become a crime. She had taken pleasure and pride in 'her' children; many of them came from farming backgrounds and, grounded in a discipline of hard work, three had made it to Oxford. Until recently, they had still sent Hermione Christmas cards with religious themes.

Looking at her friend across the kitchen table that final time, Observa had thought, 'She's aged well. She looks young enough to be my granddaughter, though she must be in her early eighties.' The etched smile lines on her face were evidence of a contented life.

Hermione had brought some thrice-drained dregs of her special green tea and some butterless dry biscuits; she was trying to pretend that things were still as they used to be. She endeavoured to put succour into the well-worn leaves with water from the butt that held Observa's intermittent water supply: cold tea was now the norm.

As they sat at the table, they both saw the shadow cross the window. A voice called, 'Hello, anyone there?' It was almost a command and not a local voice.

They did not immediately recognise Kylie. Her family owned a second home, which they seldom used, on the outer fringes of the parish and she had walked the five miles to see whether there was any one left.

Under normal circumstances, Kylie and Hermione would never have thought of spending time together because they were so different. Kylie's father was a famous DJ, of whom Observa and Hermione had never heard, who had made his fortune by being a 'celeb'. That word was not in the old dictionaries but had been made flesh in the twenty-first century, though it was yet to be understood by country folk. For Kylie and her father, celebrity opened doors and they exuded an aura of entitlement; their word was 'The Word'.

These offcomers had made little effort to integrate into village life. They had got off on the wrong foot by assuming that the fields around their retreat existed for their enjoyment and were not a source of food production and someone else's livelihood.

Observa wished she had made more effort to get to know them, but there she was again on familiar territory, blaming herself.

When roused, Hermione could be quite outspoken but she never took offence; those who tried to be offensive were dismissed with an, 'Oh dear, I am sorry you feel that way.' She had grown her own vegetables for years and kept the village supplied: courgettes, leeks and beetroot in autumn and winter; rhubarb, beans, spinach, tomatoes, salads and strawberries in spring and summer.

It was rumoured that she had never owned a television set; on fine evenings when everyone was settling down to *Eastenders* she could be seen walking the hedgerows and fences collecting remnants of sheep's wool that had been torn from fleeces by thorns and barbed wire. Some fleece hairs bore traces of coloured ruddle, the red, blue, green and orange evidence of their former owners. Hermione spun the wool and knitted it into mittens and rugs.

Observa suspected that Hermione and Kylie had never conversed, apart from a casual 'hello' or 'good morning' in passing. Kylie was in her late teens, half a century younger than Hermione, and thought to be a spoiled brat by those villagers who had met her family.

She took her instructions for life from her social-media influencer who was with her every minute of the day, throbbing from the hip pocket of her blue jeans, an app image camouflaged behind yellow pancake makeup and pouting, plastic-filled lips blowing kisses of mock affection.

Kylie was well-schooled by her influencer in the art of taking offence and she knew that she must only accept approbation from strangers. Whenever she bought a new pair of shoes – which was frequently – she felt that they didn't belong to her until she had posted a picture of them on Facebook and received at least a hundred likes in the first five minutes.

She truly believed that the increased incidence of sexually transmitted diseases was the direct result of government underfunding. Egged on by her influencer, she had in the past responded to the social media call of a local group of animal rights' saboteurs. Although she was known not to like animals, other than those labelled 'cute', she had accepted the free transport and the thirty quid on offer to don a balaclava.

The target that weekend had been the kennels of an

historic Lakeland foot pack of foxhounds – or, more exactly, the octogenarian huntsman, dear old Thomas, who lived alongside his hounds. He had kept the pack together in the hope that one day they would be allowed once more to do what they had been bred for and enjoyed.

Thomas was respected for his knowledge of nature; the four seasons were engrained in his gnarled weather-beaten hands and the earth embedded beneath his fingernails.

Kylie had had no idea who her new companions were, but they seemed to know her name as she clambered into the minivan and they welcomed her like a long-lost friend. Behind their balaclavas, Kylie couldn't tell whether they were male or female. They all carried tins of paint spray, batons and video cameras, and it had all been a bit of a laugh.

Afterwards the video went viral and funds for the 'cause' poured in. The video had not recorded old Thomas having a heart attack as he tried to protect his home and his hounds. Observa heard of his death on the grapevine and there was a short obituary in the local newspaper, though its circulation was already dwindling.

The fact that the daughter of a celeb was involved hit the headlines. Kylie appeared as a victim on the news, clutching two 'rescued' puppies, her image transposed onto a backdrop of Thomas's small living space with its cluttered, shabby Victorian furniture and iron range. On the wall was a bevelled mirror in its heavy dark-mahogany frame; it had belonged to his grandmother and it was rumoured that John Peel may have looked at it to check his neckerchief and grey coat. Now it echoed a different message in red paint: *ANIMAL MURDERERS SCUM.*

Observa would have liked to challenge Kylie, to suggest that the hounds might be happier running free on the high fells following a scent rather than becoming couch companions to humans.

Without her phone for reference, Kylie had nothing to say. Perhaps that was for the best because Observa had no wish to spend her last days on earth in acrimony.

They were odd bedfellows, thrown together at the end, trying to regain a sense of purpose and retrieve some sort of certainty. Hermione's moral compass was firmly set and still giving a positive reading, but the pointer on Kylie's had broken years ago. It was quivering in the wrong direction and there was no one left to whom she could take it in to be repaired and reset.

The three women said their goodbyes not in words but in expressions, each wanting to be among familiar surroundings with their own thoughts when the end came.

Kylie had been so certain that none of this was happening that she was convinced that when she returned to her bedroom the Wi-Fi would be working, the electricity on again. 'They' would have fixed it, though she had no idea who 'they' were.

On her way back she ignored the abandoned cars, their last drops of fuel consumed. Some contained drivers, their skeletal hands still grasping the steering wheels.

When she got home, she would charge her battery and chat to her influencer. She could still hear birds singing so all must be well, and she would ignore the cry of the hounds in the distance.

Hermione shrugged her shoulders; she was hoping to find a clump of sorrel to take the edge off her hunger. She'd had a good life and now she would go home, wrap herself in rugs and play games with her mind until she finally drifted away. She had avoided giving Kylie a hug.

It had been the afternoon of that same day when Observa walked unsteadily up to the top gate to say her goodbyes to Planet Earth. She was determined to make it whilst she still had the strength, and Reginald Heber's words were ringing in her ears: 'Where every prospect pleases and only man is vile'. She had outlived her four-score years and ten; now appeared to be a judicious moment to bid farewell and give thanks for the good times. It was time for a new start.

Her plan had been to return to the house and snuggle down among the duvets and blankets to await the end; she had not been expecting an altercation with the gate. In that final hour her plans had changed: she would die of cold, not hunger.

'God,' she thought as she lay there, 'how I could do with a whisky.' Her doctor had warned her not to use alcohol to warm herself for it could have the opposite effect, but she remembered how the old family doctor was given a bottle of single malt at Christmas when he came in for the traditional pre-lunch drink on Boxing Day.

Those deep-seated pleasantries of her youth were giving her warmth. Again she felt the heat, saw the roaring glow from the fire as the stoker smiled when she thanked him and the engine driver for a safe journey, and on Father's instructions pressed a shilling into an oily hand.

Giving a bottle nowadays had come to represent a bribe to get you to the top of the waiting list, and the warmth of coal was forbidden in order to save the planet, but at least everyone had smiled back then.

Where had all that underbelly of hate and unhappiness come from, and how had it taken hold? Was it when they started cancelling books and tried to control what you could say?

To Observa, it had all happened before in another country, which was one of the disadvantages of having lived too long. She remembered going to the cinema to see *Snow White and the Seven Dwarfs*; before the main film there was the Gaumont British News in black and white, the familiar strident music and clipped staccato voice with its Received Pronunciation. 'Schoolchildren in their fascist brown shirts, wearing their swastika armbands, burning books in the school playground under the watchful eye of their teachers.' Was burning books any worse than banning them?

Observa knew that she had outlived her stay; in less than a century it had all come round again, but this time nearer to home. But the past was another place and they did things rationally there.

She had been wrong to imagine that death would obliterate her worries; physically it had, and her heart no longer pumped heavily with anxiety, but that pain had been replaced by an over-active conscience that gnawed at her constantly.

How long would it take her to find family members in this vastness? Their souls could be anywhere. And should by some miracle any of them survived, she could no longer help them.

She wondered how she would appear to them – she had no wish to alarm them, to manifest as an apparition and scare the living daylights out of the great-grandchildren. The last time she had spoken to any of them, those three generations who came after her, the oldest were still trying to hang on to the greasy pole of ambition, just about coping at the top of their professions but feeling their hands slipping.

Observa had no desire to rekindle her earthly anxiety for them, and as for the little ones, the great-grandchildren, she could only pray that their end had come swiftly and with gentleness.

Tears no longer flowed but the agony wrenched at her soul. She tried to think of the happy times when, as toddlers, her grandchildren and great-grandchildren were captured on smartphones experiencing a few seconds of joy: a two-year-old finding his feet and becoming aware of rhythm, his body responding to the music in the background, letting himself go and releasing his soul.

It had been Fred alighting on that grubby Fountains Abbey tea towel that had brought back memories of the girls. Perhaps she would allow herself a little peek back into their childhoods and seek out the happy times.

Her daughters were so different in their ambitions, one liking her sandwiches trimmed and her potatoes mashed, the other eating up the crusts of life and throwing decorum to the winds as she stretched over the dining-room table with her fork to spear the abandoned skins of baked potatoes from the others' plates with a, 'You don't mind, do you? I can't bear to see anything go to waste.'

No, it would be best to leave well alone, because the happy times may have been fewer than she remembered or liked to imagine.

✳

She knew that she must be more adventurous and stop hovering near to the ground, stop thinking that hanging on would still offer a type of security. The cancer of indecision and uncertainty still dominated her mind; would she really have to spend eternity convinced that all the decisions she had made in life had been the wrong ones?

She wondered who she might bump into. It was unlikely to be anyone really interesting like Stephen Hawkins, Bertrand Russell, George Orwell or Bob Dylan because they would surely be in a more rarefied orbit, their minds on a different level. Even so, they must be around somewhere because Observa had read that they had all experienced last-minute conversions on the road to Damascus.

Anyway, she would be out of her depth in their

company, wouldn't know what to say. And if there were extra-terrestrial beings of a higher intelligence, it would be better to leave them to it and not try to pretend she had anything in common with them. She had tried to do that on Earth and it hadn't worked; she recalled the palpable sneering of those who felt themselves superior to her. A mere look could convey thoughts, and those withering put-downs had convinced Observa to stand back, even if, by doing so she attracted comments that she was a bit standoffish.

There had been that other visionary in Observa's day, a scholar and statesmen who was misunderstood and vilified; perhaps she would bump into him. He might need a soulmate to whom he could get things off his chest. He had understood the human psyche and how it might behave when finally put to the test; like too many chickens crammed into a small coop, people would peck at each other.

As the great exodus of people from their desert homelands had moved north, he had tried to give a warning but the words he used were from another age and not recognised in the twenty-first century. Fires were lit and mistrust had been the phoenix that had risen from the ashes. What had he been called? Once his name had been on everyone's lips. Was he not the eldest son of Cain's brother and the father of Methuselah?

Humankind had been persuaded to let go of the tiller and drifted out to sea, their destination irreversible. It was just like that time in her teens when Observa was staying with Prue for half-term to escape from the ghastliness of boarding school. Prue's father, an Oxford blue, had introduced her to sculling against the strong currents of the River Severn. Observa had been confident that her ability to row a boat on the mill pond of Ullswater would enable her to master the unfamiliar scull and strong river currents, so she was shocked when the oar was pulled from her hand. Now independent of her, it took its own course and disappeared. From time to time it re-emerged and she had glimpsed it amid the tossing waves until it was lost from view round a far bend downstream.

✳

Was Jesus still sitting patiently on the Mount of Olives like in old times, trying to warn people, even though He must know it was too late? The cedars of Lebanon were being splintered by gunfire all around Him. The peace of God that passeth all understanding had not clicked with the general public; the time for excuses was over and accounts must be settled.

Observa thought again about Prue. Their friendship had lasted almost ninety years; there had been separations and reunions over the years and then that final visit.

Prue had phoned to say she would be in the Lakes and Northumberland visiting old friends, and Observa had offered her a bed for the night. They had spent a pleasant day together and visited some of the places they had shared in their youth: Ullswater, Deepdale and Gowbarrow.

The reminiscences and laughter and giggles from their

teenage years had lasted into the evening. They were enjoying a pre-supper drink when Prue had said, 'I've got a bit of bad news. Last week—'

At that moment Observa's phone had rung and she had hurried to answer it with a, 'Sorry, won't be a tick.' But she had been more than a tick because the voice at the other end was giving her exciting news. 'Congratulations, you have won the Poetry Prize and your poem will be published in our forthcoming anthology.'

Approbation on the academic front was so rare in Observa's life that she wanted to hold the person on the line for ever, but she was also anxious to share it with Prue, her clever, clever friend with a first in languages who had not lived up to her scholastic promise.

Observa had been so obsessed with her own good news that Prue's bad news had never seen the light of day. It had been revealed, however, three weeks after her visit when Prue's husband, Pete, had phoned to say that Prue had died of cancer and had been pleased to have had the chance to say goodbye to all her northern friends.

Observa's feelings of guilt re-emerged. The chance to make amends with Prue had gone forever, she and her family had been staunch disbelievers.

She wondered if the meaning of words had changed in Heaven as they had on earth, those words that once gave comfort now misinterpreted and causing offence, universally spewed from the lips of people and iPads with nothing of value to say, 'isms' tossed like black confetti to smother and choke reasoned debate and destroy happiness.

Observa had searched for the word happiness in the dictionary; it said pleasure and good fortune, but what she was really searching for was contentment and definitions that would ease her mind. The young had abandoned the goal of contentment and replaced it with a sense of entitlement; with the click of a button they demanded instant satisfaction and a transitory fix of happiness.

When the lights finally went out and the TV screens were flickering their death throes, there were no anchor persons left to feed their false messages. Eros was already in the shadows, the familiar neon lights on the billboards surrounding Piccadilly Circus the last to go, their relentless message of *SALE SALE SALE* joined by *'everything now up for grabs, don't miss the bargain of a lifetime'* until the letters became erratic. *ALE* and *SAS* appeared briefly before complete darkness fell and finally all men became equal.

In a way, the levelling up had already started: Asian bedbugs had been reported infesting The Ritz, and the Penthouse at the Dorchester had been fumigated.

CHAPTER 9

Observa couldn't get the tune or the words out of her head, nor could she remember when she had first heard them. 'I want to be where everyone knows my name'; it was one of those American eighties' comedies, repeated again and again when people still laughed at themselves.

She assumed she must now be among friends, but there were those with whom she still felt she needed to make amends. There was that clever couple – what was their name and why had she suddenly thought of them? – a husband and wife with whom it had been difficult to break the ice.

Both were medics doing research, something to do with neuroscience at Liverpool University, and Observa had shared the school run with them. Misunderstandings had arisen that were still to be put right.

It had happened shortly before the couple had moved from the area, and it had left Observa with her guilt. She tried to remember the conversations they had exchanged, other than those connected to the school run and general chit-chat about children.

Inwardly she had felt sorry for Joyce's children –
Joyce, yes that was her name. Having brilliant parents
was always a disadvantage if the children did not carry
the clever genes or the physically attractive ones of their
begetters.

Poor little Philippa, with her porky looks, thick-lensed
glasses and loving nature, struggling with the obligatory
maths, unable to live up to her mother's racy sports-car
image and sensing maternal disappointment. The boy
had been handsome and quiet, but first impressions could
cloud perception.

Observa had plucked up courage and asked them round
for a meal. It had not taken place in the kitchen, clutching
a mug and enjoying the informality of the cluttered table,
but in the stuffy dining room among the silver and all
that fetching and carrying when conversation became
difficult.

She could not remember the exact order of Joyce's
words but they had been to the effect that 'the time will
come when we have only to think ourselves in a place in
order to be there'.

In those days it had been easier to believe in the afterlife
and the resurrection. The taboo subject of God had come
up and there had been awkward pauses as Observa had
carefully tried to choose her words.

'Don't you think it's a bit arrogant of humans to believe
that there is no greater presence than themselves?'

The answer had been swift. 'Poppycock! Science is the
answer to everything.'

Now, so many years later, Observa thought about those

Nobel Laureates, those ageing Silicon Valley billionaires with their young trophy wives trying to forestall physical deterioration, injecting themselves with plasma taken from their offspring, confident that their money would buy them immortality.

Hugh had never particularly liked Joyce, but that was his attitude to all clever women; he had tolerated her because of the school run. But he had agreed with her statement.

Observa had been outnumbered on the subject of faith, though she believed that a kindly God would open the pearly gates for Hugh in the end and give him dispensation. Eventually she would bump into him again – but she was in no hurry to do so and until then she would enjoy her freedom.

But she would never have an opportunity to right that misunderstanding with Joyce; she and her husband Gordon had made it clear that they were both active members of the secular society and non-starters in the Heaven stakes.

Atonement was becoming a bit of a problem; surely the afterlife was not going to be a regurgitation of life's mistakes with little chance of putting things right? That misunderstanding with Joyce had been petty but had run deep.

Observa had always been afraid that her body language sent out the wrong message and she thought of Robbie Burns, just across the border: 'Oh to see ourselves as others see us.'

To recognise, understand and forgive the frailty of

others took a lifetime; to recognise it in oneself took even longer. Now her life was over, Observa's past was nagging away continually, not allowing her to forget.

Dementia would have been a blessing.

✳

She had been looking out of an upstairs window; the children would be home soon and it was Joyce's turn for the school run. She saw the car arrive and the children get out.

Joyce saw her and waved but appeared in no hurry to drive off; she looked as though she were refreshing her lipstick. Perhaps Observa should have gone downstairs and said hello, but Joyce usually gave the impression that she had better things to do – off to a tennis lesson or a seminar – so Observa had convinced herself that the woman would not want to be held up.

That evening the phone had rung. Before Observa had time for the usual pleasantries, Joyce had waded in. 'What is it with you? You're so standoffish. You never come out for a chat, you just wave like Lady Muck.'

Observa remembered feeling physically sick, and the words of her eldest brother had come back to her.

They'd been children, squabbling on the back seat of the old bull-nosed Morris. They had been on a day out with father to witness the spectacle of the becks in full spate as they roared down from the high fells after weeks of torrential rain. At Lodore Falls in Borrowdale, the peaty foaming waters ricocheted off the huge boulders and the gentle misty spray refreshed their faces.

Father had looked at his watch and said that the bar would be open now so they must leave the magic behind. Returning home on the twisty lakeside road running parallel to Derwentwater, they had spotted a small group of birds far out on the lake, silhouetted against the horizon and too distant to identify.

Observa had said, 'Ooh, look, geese!'

Her brother had snapped, 'They're not geese, you idiot! They're swans,' and a minor argument had ensued. It had ended up with her brother saying, 'I feel sorry for anyone who marries you.'

She had taken the insult as she always did; as the only female sibling, she had learned to laugh them off. But that evening, holding the telephone and listening to Joyce, she'd heard it again.

A pill was yet to be discovered that could obliterate memory. Smartphones had been doing a pretty good job but Observa had always stuck to her trusted 'cream of the barley' and its pleasurable 40% proof.

In the end her elder brother's swans had all turned out to be geese and he'd lived an optimistic and impecunious life. Observa had envied him.

✳

Had she been born a hundred years later, she could have tried transgendering but knew she would not have been happy with that either because she had, as the female chorus had sung in the 1950s' musical *South Pacific* 'enjoyed being a girl'.

Trying to be assertive didn't become her. She felt that her mind inhabited a world of abstract concepts, a phrase she had heard on BBC4. It had seemed to fit at the time.

Observa had once welcomed the rise of feminism, flirted with it as she tried to stand up to her brothers, but she had finally learnt to keep her own counsel. The vociferousness and aggression of her sisters alarmed her; the female of the species had quickly turned out to be far deadlier than the male. Abandoning femininity and scorning chivalry, they had acquired all the bad traits of male manipulation whilst destroying all the attractive qualities of masculinity.

In her day, men smelt of men; it was part of their physical attraction. They had understood the power of a crowbar and how to use it. Now they hadn't the strength to lift one off the ground; instead they smothered themselves in eau de Cologne as if they were putting on a female repellent.

Thousands of years of evolution had been obliterated in a couple of decades – there had even been programmes on the telly about how to be a man.

As glass ceilings were shattered and boardrooms taken over, the whiff of Mammon grew stronger. Hard-faced, unsmiling women now sat in the chairman's seat at the AGMs of international companies, welcoming shareholders, basking in applause and their salaries as financial statements were read out and the credit given to AI.

'This wonderful technology will enable your company

to have access to everyone, to target the healthy and vulnerable, persuade them that our products are vital for their well-being, forewarn them of the dangers of not using precautionary medicines.'

Observa had almost expected to hear the words 'let's put the fear of God into them'. Profit graphs became impressive, the line almost vertical, everyone clapped and the champagne corks popped.

She had been pleased to leave all that behind, but there had been periods of joy that she longed to recapture. Those early days of spring when overnight the miracle that was nature changed its colour and you awoke to the sun, its warmth throwing a verdant blanket across the fields and bringing the hedgerows to life, creating white criss-cross patterns and patchworks of blossom and renewed hope and harmony.

Nature was so certain of itself; it didn't need a referendum or a general election. When change became necessary, dandelions replaced the daffodils. Solomon in all his glory had not been arrayed like one of these.

Thank God I'm dead, she thought. I made it just in time, before contentment became a thing of the past and uncertainty took over. The family had laid bets on her living to a hundred but there was no one left to collect the winnings.

With eternity stretching ahead, there should be no difficulty in making contact with her daughters in her own good time. Although she had no wish to disturb their newly found peace of mind, when the time came she knew exactly where she would find her first born. Conceived in innocence and a sense of duty, she would be in that place where she found her contentment by satisfying her thirst for knowledge, that snug little corner of the Bodleian with the north-facing window. If she was in luck, the comfortable old leather armchair which she called her own would be unoccupied and waiting for her.

Her sister, the result of passion a decade later, would be more difficult to locate. In life she had always been going places, jumping on a plane at a moment's notice and going where a whim and an offer of a cheap flight took her, encountering one of those pockets of the planet's isolated, indigenous people, survivors who had escaped the 'benefits' of European civilisation.

CHAPTER 10

In those last months, a few people had still been around trying to believe that the end of the world was not really upon them but knowing that it was. There had been so many false alarms; people had cried wolf for centuries.

Observa remembered the Hyde Park Corner placards of her youth that stated *The End Is Nigh*. They had been premature by half a century, but she had heard the whisperings then and she should have listened. Now it was too late; she had not done all those things she ought to have done, but she had done all those things she ought not to have done. If the general confession was to be taken at its word, there was no health in her.

And so it appeared to have turned out. Even those causes that she had taken up in the autumn of her life and felt good about had turned into paper tigers or confirmed her suspicions that she had backed the wrong horse.

Neighbours had sat at her kitchen table, trying to say the right thing, 'Is this it, then?' and waiting to go their separate ways. Each of them was carrying the weight of life's baggage, those bundles of should haves and shouldn't haves, those kindnesses left undone that could have been so easily accomplished.

At one of those last kitchen-table gatherings, when the final solution was being discussed, Esme had arrived. Esme had been a lifelong *Guardian* reader and normally her conversation was doom laden and finger pointing.

Observa had classified her as a clicker, never happier than when she was giving her opinion about something she had never witnessed. Incapable of debate or thinking things through, Esme fed off the opinions of others. She was yet to appoint an influencer, but her forefinger went into overdrive to select the correct link to change government policy and she had quickly become an expert in everything.

Observa had learnt to keep quiet in her presence, say nothing unless to comment about the weather and admire the blossom. There had been two or three times when Esme had felt she was losing an argument and walked off in a huff, slamming the door and cracking the plaster on the kitchen wall. Observa had brushed it off. What was a bit of door slamming between friends?

She knew that the certainty of her own memories was now disallowed, *verboten*, a remembered word from when they had played at Nazis as children and ridiculed Hitler. Eighty years later, it was no longer a game; the world had capitulated to a fifth column, a Trojan horse bearing the name Mr Mawkish, its sire Human Rights out of Miss Sentimentality.

That day Esme had been uncharacteristically optimistic. 'What about the Inuits living on the fringe of the North

Pole? They will still be alive, isolated and self-sufficient.'

Esme was a vegan and into animal rights, and Observa did not wish to disillusion her in her last hours, but had she not seen the nature programme about survival in Alaska? The Inuits lived entirely on seal and polar-bear meat; each community had permission from the Alaskan government to shoot three polar bears a year for their meat and, more importantly, their fur.

No, Esme had not seen it. 'I don't watch those programmes, too brutal. I prefer Chris Packham wearing one of his reassuring primrose or pink polystyrene body warmers.'

Observa had not responded. Instead she had said, 'We should accept that there is a greater power than ourselves and He is in charge now.'

In true *Guardian* fashion, Esme had retorted, 'How do you know He's a he?'

'Well, it's not our worry now.' Observa had tried to placate her, but in her mind she was trying to authenticate something she had read in Isaiah about the lion lying down with the lamb.

Could the animal rights people be right? She had tried to find the answer by Googling the quote, but first it had been necessary to click something that would give her information about how to buy a Volvo car so she had given up.

Hermione, the peacekeeper who read *Country Life* and who was aware of Observa's seniority, had turned to her. 'We value your wisdom,' she'd said.

It was far too late to value anything, though it was nice

to be acknowledged even at this late hour. And Observa had thought, 'Holy Moses, what on earth have I done to deserve this? Why are they asking me?'

If her memories were to be believed, she should be the last person on earth to be asked for an opinion. Through every aspect of her life, she had carried self-doubt and lived in a state of perpetual penitence.

The psychologists had recently given how she felt a name, 'existential anxiety', but she disliked having her emotions classified; she preferred the old way of having a good scream and smashing a few plates. Mother had kept a stack handy, just in case, though with Father they had been unnecessary.

Anyway, hadn't it been sorted all those years ago in the Garden of Eden? She remembered her letters to *The Times*, written and never sent, languishing in drafts on her computer.

She thought of Father again. He had taught her to recognise the beauty and cruelty of nature, taught her to accept and respect both its nice and nasty sides and not to make judgements about anything until you had experienced it first-hand. But nature and reality had been usurped.

Observa knew that she had outstayed her welcome on this earth by at least fifteen years. There was no one left to corroborate the past – it really was another country, its borders now closed and its inhabitants speaking in a different tongue.

Anyway, her passport was out of date; it had expired before her.

When Observa had said what she believed, tried to impart her faith and pass on the reassuring words she had heard as a child, she could tell what her listeners were thinking: 'bit of an oddball here'.

Before the end had come, her great-grandchildren were already being questioned about their faith and teased at school. Christianity was no longer top of the pops.

Other conversations came drifting back. 'The problem is that humans have become arrogant, and arrogance is begot by ignorance.' Esme was quoting something she'd probably read in the *New Statesman*.

'Well, I hope you don't think me ignorant! Accept and understand the frailty in others, lest they see ours.'

Observa could no longer remember who had said what.

*

Reuben had been the last man to come to her table. Although it was over eighty years since they had last seen one another, their first encounter had forged a lifelong bond of understanding undimmed by time.

It was no surprise that he had tracked her down for he was of true Romany stock and had retained instincts and senses long abandoned and left to wither by civilised man.

Their bond had been created when he was still a child and Observa was just old enough to have been his mother. She had always known that she would find him again for he lay hidden somewhere in her mind, so circumstances would draw them together again magnetically.

He must have been five or six years old when he first came, wise beyond his years, brought by his traveller family to the Appleby horse fair. He was barefoot astride a black-and-white cob, riding bareback with the silky coat of the horse between his legs.

He had walked the east fellside with his grandmother, through the villages of Murton, Dufton and Knock where those fairy mountains, the Pikes, had stood sentinel for millennia and guarded the Eden valley below. For centuries the songs of skylark and curlew and the bleat of lambs had been the only sound echoing off their escarpments, but eventually the drum-drum-drumming of wheels on the A66 had drowned all that melody.

It was said thereabouts that when God had created the Pennines the three Pikes had been the three handfuls of earth left over from His initial creation. Reuben had grown up with that myth, told to him by his grandmother, and he'd never had reason to doubt it; his own experience confirmed that the elements, not mankind, were in charge.

He had learned early that there were kind and unkind people and you had to take the rough with the smooth. He looked forward to going round the villages with his grandmother, selling their wares of handmade wooden clothes pegs and sprigs of lucky heather. His grandmother had shown Reuben how to leave a message for other travellers that here they would be welcome, its message understood only by those of the travelling communities. It was a small scratch mark on the sandstone gatepost that said, 'Here be friends.'

That last time, she had seen him approaching the house, his stride purposeful and sprightly. She'd known instantly that it was him. She had opened the door to him before he had a chance to knock and they had embraced. The thick, coarse, hand-knitted woollen that engulfed him smelled of sheep. The years had disappeared and there he was, a child again, and she was sitting by the Eden watching him take the cob into the water for its traditional swim and wash. The trust between horse and boy was complete as his bare legs squeezed its flanks to guide and reassure it.

She remembered Father's words of instruction when he had first lifted her onto a horse – she must have been about three. 'You only need two things to communicate with him, your voice and leg pressure. They are all that are necessary.'

To make certain she understood about the leg pressure, Father had placed a penny coin between Observa's knees and the pony's flank. 'Keep the pressure on at all times. If the penny falls, you are not in communication with the horse.'

Reuben had not needed pennies.

Perhaps he had been sent as a messenger, a guide, She heard again the momentary splash of water against the horse's shoulder, in an instant gone on its journey to the sea to pass all those places Father had so loved.

From her lofty position, she could look down, follow in her mind's eye the twists and turns of the river. Somewhere along the way Father would be there in his waders, rod in hand.

CHAPTER 11

She would start at Pooley Bridge, stand again on the medieval hump-backed packhorse bridge of her youth, its sandstone strength laboured from the local quarry. It had been swept to its death by Storm Desmond and replaced by a new, wider, slicker bridge constructed in foreign stone – with traffic lights.

Now Observa could visit the old one again, take herself back, stand in the niche of one of its central buttresses, the demarcation line of two counties. Legs astride, she looked downstream, her left foot planted firmly in Cumberland and her right foot in Westmorland; turn around and face Ullswater's oncoming waters, and your feet changed county.

Father had delighted in imparting this obvious knowledge to generations of children. The magic had been destroyed with the building of the new bridge. For no apparent reason the County Council had declared that historic boundary lines must be altered, and children no longer knew where to place their feet.

But the lake was constant; it knew where it was going,

channelling and transforming its waters into a river to travel downstream, anxious to be away.

The rock was still just below the bridge, breaking the water's flow. Observa's brothers and cousins had raced to reach it, stripped off and waded or swum to crown themselves kings of the castle. Away from adult jurisdiction, they had stretched out on their backs on its flat surface, hands behind their heads.

They were always first, bagging the best place. There was only room for two so they'd pushed Observa back into the water with their feet as she'd tried to clamber up. People from the bridge waved and called, and she had accepted that there was no room for her; she would have to wait until she was welcome.

As she hovered over the rock, which was now almost fully submerged, she liked to imagine that Christ was still sitting patiently on His rock on the Mount of Olives, wearily trying to have His say and looking more and more like John Lennon as the days passed. He had to accept that a new beginning was necessary – and pretty quickly before His Father's masterplan festered and the meaning of life was forgotten.

God had tried to give people a get-out clause, an excuse for their bad behaviour. 'And ye shall hear of wars and rumours of wars; see that ye be not troubled; for all these things must come to pass.' Mankind had to hit rock bottom before redemption could be considered, but patience was not always a good thing.

*

It was difficult to identify some of the places where she thought Father might be, where they had shared contentment. In her mind's eye, Observa was following the river Eamont; shortly it would join forces with the Lowther, and in few miles would swing west after converging with the Eden at rivers' meet. Then on to Langwathby and its old medieval sandstone bridge, anxious to reach the sea and see where the pull of the moon might take its waters. Who knew where? Maybe they would lap the shores of Nova Scotia or South America or, if they encountered the jet stream, Scandinavia.

In the meantime, Observa was trying to recall the names of the places where contentment lay – Honey Pot, Dolphenby and Udford – inaccessible places that had been worth the walk, carrying picnics and fishing tackle in search of a day of peace and quiet and togetherness.

✳

She was certain that she could feel a presence, someone trying to make contact.

'Is it you, Gobby?' A child's voice from the past, a childhood rearranged by war; it was one of the many evacuees her parents had welcomed into their home. Those children had witnessed for the first time the possibility of a different existence from the back-to-back slums of the East End of London; there was a paradise waiting to be found.

Could it be Jimmy, the ten year old whom father had so loved, taken under his wing and treated as one of his own? He had taught the boy the ways of the countryside, how to fish and shoot rabbits for the pot.

When the time came to go home, when the hostilities of war had ceased, Jimmy had rebelled. He did not want to return with his family and he had clung to Father, weeping.

Observa could see now that you only needed to believe strongly enough that you were in a place to be there. Clever, clever, clever Joyce of the school run had been right in her predictions after all: there really was such a thing as a time machine.

As she rounded the final corner before the river straightened, she saw Langwathby bridge in the distance. She had expected the left bank to be as she remembered it, a vertical, treeless sandbank pitted with the homes of kingfishers, but the river had widened to accommodate the merging waters. Only scrub was visible.

She raised her eyes, hoping to see the old bridge, but it had disappeared and in its place was a metal military construction. False promises had been made to rebuild the old bridge after it was swept away in the1960s, but after half a century those promises had faded.

As she looked more closely, something caught her eye on the far side of the river five or six feet from the shore. Where the high, wooded hill cascaded its trees and bushes into the river, she saw a familiar figure, half submerged, brown trilby, pipe in mouth, casting downstream, the line stretched to where the trout were rising.

Something made him turn his head. He saw her and called out as though he had been expecting her, and she crossed the river because now she could walk on water.

There was no greeting as he handed her the rod. 'Here, you have a go. They've been rising under the pool by the willow tree. Jimmy was here earlier.'

Observa took the rod and cast it, the flick of her wrist instinctive, The whirr of the reel was familiar and reassuring; the line caressed the surface of the water and settled gently when it reached the willow tree. She felt the slightest tug.

Father said, 'That was a perfect cast.' His arm went round her shoulders. 'You haven't lost your touch.'

www.ingramcontent.com/pod-product-compliance
Lightning Source LLC
Chambersburg PA
CBHW040231170726
48295CB00014B/880